Search for the Grail

By

Brian Grant

PublishAmerica
Baltimore

ISBN: 978-1-4489-2140-9
PUBLISHED BY PUBLISHAMERICA, LLLP
www.publishamerica.com
Baltimore

Printed in the United States of America

SEARCH FOR THE GRAIL

Synopsis

It seemed to Garth Pilgrim that his life had reached its end, when his wife died of cancer, her relations blamed him for her death because of the pressure he threw upon her, the stress relating to his imprisonment for the killing of a colleague while investigating corrupt politicians as an M I 6 agent. A letter arrives from Chip by the morning post, a good friend whom he met while in prison, asking Pilgrim to attend a meeting with a wheelchair bound character called Tobias Levy; Pilgrim is thankful for the invitation.

A chauffeured car whisks them away to this appointment, but instead of the expected destination of Mayfair London, they travel north arriving in Grantham as night falls. It is a large Victorian mansion with domed roofs and spiralling towers, shrouded in drifting mist; exuding a fearful mystic ambience.

The promised financial rewards offered for the search, to find certain individuals by this proposed employer is staggering, it is impossible for the friends to know this harmless looking bespectacled individual sitting in a wheelchair; is a pernicious Devil-worshipping fanatic seeking ownership of the Holy Grail!

Pilgrim is shocked to be told by this man during a conversation, that he is aware of his absolute innocence of the crime he was imprisoned for; these few words inevitably leading him to a revealing truth. The two friends on this adventure are drawn along a trail of decadence and iniquity; they are faced with situations beyond their wildest nightmares. Inadvertently,978-1-4489-2140-9 they manage to find their true paths in life through the arcane radiance of the Holy Grail, which carries them through this heart stopping oddesy.

CHAPTER 1
The Blindfolding of Nemesis!

John Tregear was careful to stand in the shadows of the roadside foliage, hopefully hidden away from the powerful revealing head lights of passing cars, he regrettably was very conscious of the pain accompanying heavy blood loss from the bullet wound in his shoulder. The special agent did manage to cleverly evade the clutches of his pursuers, although several shots were fired at him, but fortunately or possibly unfortunately only one damaged his left shoulder!

Tregear was a fit young tall dark haired intelligent M I 6 agent, who at this particular moment while suffering with a bullet wound in his shoulder, was trying not to think about his beloved young wife or their future; as he was now realising how deep the inquiries were probing to create these violent reactions. The major question he asked himself was—how the hell did they know anything about this ongoing covert investigation; when only he and his colleague Pilgrim were involved?

Trigger as he liked to be called, was the working colleague of Garth Pilgrim; both of them young operational M I 6 agents. Trigger had arranged for Pilgrim, to join him outside this property called "The One Tree House," in Furzehill avenue, one of the affluent tree-lined avenue's of Hampstead London; as the man who lived there was under very close observation.

He was cold—realising it was through the heavy loss of blood, plus he was feeling more than a little irritable and very concerned about this entire operation, as well as his and Pilgrim's safety; even his wife questioned him about his morose attitude! The house being watched was the residence of a junior minister, respectfully called: *The Right Honourable Robin Wenham MP*. While John Tregear with his colleague Garth Pilgrim both M I 6 agents, were on the trail of something so big, it was now beginning, to make them feel more than fearful of the consequences; if they handled it incorrectly.

Wenham's reputation for honest dealings with large government contracts is at this moment definitely in question, Pilgrim received an anonymous phone call some six months ago, pertinently revealing complete details of enormous civil contracts worth billions of pounds, infiltrated by international criminals with the full cooperation of certain top politicians.

.Obviously this person who made the call was a civil servant seriously concerned for his own safety, desperately wanting to remain anonymous; this fortuitous message set Pilgrim with his colleague Trigger on the trail like bloodhounds. They were at first duty bound to investigate the claims made by this unknown caller, which they did in a rather pragmatic manner, more than dubiously unbelieving these outrageous accusations; but the further they dug into the pile of supplied manure—the more incriminating evidence was uncovered!

Seemingly this man Wenham, whose house he had been watching for several hours in the darkness of this evening's sporadic rainfall, was one of the leading participants. Wenham was also closely linked with another very senior cabinet minister, called Alfred Etherington; surreptitious bank accounts belonging to both of these men were placed discreetly in the Channel Islands with several more in Liechtenstein. On these balance sheets were recorded large regular payments, these gratuities were from well known criminal members of notorious drug gangs; wanting to wash vast amounts of profits from their highly lucrative criminal activities.

As Trigger with Pilgrim probed even deeper, it became intensely obvious; these revelations would collapse this present very successful popular government, as if it were a house of cards.

Pilgrim discussed the operation in great detail with Trigger, reminding him that they were teetering on the edge of exhibiting to the nation, along with a listening watching world; a typical case of banana republic anarchy in the midst of this very proud England!

The immense power of these particular politicians, that he with Pilgrim were attacking, conjured up for both of them—nightmare visions of draconian reprisals, in pursuit of not only defiantly maintaining their veneer of pompous righteousness; but also the continued greedy flow of laundered wealth into their bulging secret accounts!

The two young agents spent three hours that very morning collating every detail of the last three months investigation, they then sealed this explosive information into several large files, to be kept in a clandestine location; just in case anything questionable happened to either of them.

Also they agreed on an agenda that they would reveal all to their senior officers on the following day, which was against Pilgrim's wishes—he wanted to notify Cunningham, the head of M I 6 immediately; but his colleague Trigger wanted another day. Trigger hoped that on the eve of the handover, it would be possible to find additional damning evidence to finalise this sensational inquiry; unknown to either of them it was a decision that was going to wreck their lives!

Trigger was now very-very cold, he wore in his ear what looked like an I-pod earpiece, but of course it was an electronic listening device tuned in to the villainous MP's telephone. They were aware this man was due to attend a meeting with his ambiguous associates that very evening, which would hopefully allow Trigger, to search the study of this crook Wenham, in the hope of finding more incriminating evidence to positively bring this long inquiry to an absolute finality; but the appointments must have changed for the MP was still in his study.

It was this uncertainty, coupled with the heavy responsibility of this entire far reaching package of corruption, which was really causing a normal stoical character like Tregear to feel a sense of fearful insecurity. Trigger pushed himself deeper into the large boundary garden hedge behind him, to again avoid the bright lights of the passing cars, grimacing at the wet leaves emptying their cold contents down his neck. When suddenly the well known defining sound of a spitting silenced revolver; sent John Tregear a loyal subject of crown and country, on an early entrance into the next world.

The assassins performed as two dark shadows, ruthlessly and unceremoniously silently dragging the young dead Trigger into the front garden of the hedged premises, leaving the sad lonely figure to lay hidden by the obscurity of darkness, only to be revealed by the honesty of dawn's first light!

Pilgrim certainly did arrive at the location, where Trigger was observing the house in question as arranged, but alas too late, only to be caught in a shocked state kneeling over the dead body of his friend and colleague; the timing of the scheming culprits absolutely precise.

There were many facets of this murder case to be considered by the investigative authorities; none of course evoked any truthful reflections. As some times happens in this very difficult world in which we all survive, circumstantial proof plus forensic evidence was procured to substantially convict Garth Pilgrim of this heinous crime!

Bearing in mind the authentic compilation of evidence against these corrupt government officials, which was now safely stowed away in a secreted cache; proof that would condemn those that had manufactured an indictment of murder! Data which would wash his good name away from this nightmare predicament—in time, but as the manufactured evidence built up—he knew he was at this moment, being forced to accept a hopeless situation. Desperately Pilgrim believed rightly so—that the public thought of him as an opprobrium; to the lay man—quote!

"A public disgrace—a man who ruthlessly killed his working colleague for no good reason." So under these aggressive degenerative attitudes of public derision towards him, containing written verbal hostilities that destroyed his social status; Pilgrim decided to keep his mouth shut. Accepting this astonishing sequence of events, knowing but also believing through his hate coupled with his personal resilience; that he would return at a later date to point his finger at those truly responsible!

There were many at the time, who felt that Nemesis the Goddess of justice and retribution was shrouded by a dark shadow, impairing her clear vision of the law; one can only hope that Father Time will perhaps intervene on behalf of the good lady; to correct this odious injustice!

CHAPTER 2
ℋ Time to Live and a Time to Die!

A lbert the local antique dealer revelled in early morning exercise, very proud of the fact that he was fit and strong for a man of his age, the dealer was very capable of running at a good pace, to complete five miles every morning around the track at this local sports centre; a pleasant oasis of deserted lush greenery. Out in front of him was a young chap, tall lithe in fact a good mover; who was always a lot faster than the middle aged man following! The younger man's name was Moses, a pleasant good looking lad, with blonde curly hair jumping about his face as he ran; they had met several times over the last week.

Moses always arriving earlier than Albert, but usually, they left together, both men finding the running common ground for a chat; as they walked back to their cars each day. The older man was always throwing in remarks concerning his work, about how he was always in town buying antiques of some sort; the training kept his brain fit and up to speed.

Albert always enjoyed the words of admiration concerning his new Jaguar, from his new found running companion. Moses explained how he worked at a desk in the city every day so he needed the exercise, after being desk bound day after day.

The dark straight haired, gaunt faced older man, had no reason to disbelieve, or even care whether or not he was telling the truth, why should he; after all he was just a passing ship in the night or in this case, a passing runner in the morning.

The antiques expert admired the youngster for being consistent, he set a cracking pace every morning, surprisingly for a younger man he was never late, which he thought in his pious way, was unusual for the youth of today. Albert smiled to himself as he stopped by his training bag, then standing with his hands on his hips, started to breathe deeply, trying to control the labouring of his lungs, encased in his tall skinny body which was sweating profusely.

The youngster lapped his running companion again, as he came from behind to stop beside the deep breathing would be athlete, stooping to pick up his towel with the water from beside the track as he spoke; his voice containing obvious traces of a strong Yorkshire accent.

"Darn nuisance, I have to be in a little earlier this morning so I need a fast car."

The boyish smile still spreading across the mischievous young face as he spoke, imitating the well spoken accent of his senior,

"Unfortunately for you Albert old chap it has to be yours."

Albert thought for a moment as he stood wiping the sweat from his face, that he had heard wrong, so he looked inquiringly at the younger man as he asked,

"I beg your pardon, what was it you needed?"

Replied Albert his well bred pronounced words seemed to ring across the field, but the young man's smile never diminished as he explained; mimicking again the Englishman's well spoken southern accent.

"The point is old chap; you had a good day yesterday, you bought something from a certain Scottish character, that wasn't meant for you. We did anticipate this happening, that's why I turned up on the scene, just as a—"

Here Moses paused before throwing emphasis on the word insurance,

"A little *insurance* as my wise old father used to say."

Albert looked at the younger man in utter astonishment desperately trying to admonish the words of the younger blonde upstart.

"I'm not really sure what you're talking about, you could not possibly mean the golden chalice, something I've been chasing all my life."

The young man's voice adopted a more serious tone as he answered,

"Oh yes I mean exactly the golden chalice, or to name it correctly; the Holy Grail! I was told to give you a chance to sell it to me, but I suspect you would never do that?"

Albert now was beginning to get really angry.

"Damned right! I would never sell it, I don't think you know what it is you're talking about you young idiot!"

The young man's grin spread from ear to ear as he answered, his face adopting again a sort of little boy'sEish look of defiance,

"Oh yes, being a good little Catholic boy I do know what it is—I've watched you carefully enough to know, you never took it from your Jaguar last night! I am now guessing that this means you intend delivering the merchandise today."

Albert was now completely bewildered, unable to take in this sudden turn of events, beginning to realise he was now in very great danger, wishing he had delivered the artefact the night before as he was supposed to have done,

"So that's why you want my car, the golden chalice?"

The young man rolled his eyes in fake sympathy as he answered,

"Oh don't get all sentimental, I like the car as well, it's just lucky for me they are both together."

Moses stooped again, this time to pick up his back pack which held all his running needs; then taking from the bag a 9MM Glock 17; with a silencer on the barrel.

"Look, if it makes you feel better, I'm sorry about this, it's just not a personal thing, I do quite like you, but I do this for a living; it's my business, you understand."

Albert's face had a look of, I don't believe what I'm hearing, being quite shocked into a moments silence before he could pull himself together, to answer this young blonde headed lunatic standing in front of him; that was holding a gun threatening to kill him!

"Surely you're not going to use that thing here right now, are you? Everybody will hear you!"

Young Moses burst out laughing,

"Everybody?"

Moses shook his head as he spoke the first few words.

"There is no everybody! The field is empty on a bright early sunny summer's morning; it's a good time to die, don't you agree?" Albert suddenly realised, he really was going to die, this was not a joke but an outright threat to his very existence, he turned quickly to make a run for it; but escape was hopeless. Four bullets spat angrily from the weapon, poor proud Albert died instantly.

Moses walked over to the slumped body to feel for the pulse at the neck, he callously fired another shot into the back of the head of the antique connoisseur, causing the body to jerk and yet more blood to flood out reddening the lush green grass.

The assassin went through the corpse's pockets to find the car key, collected his belongings then walked away leaving the body where it fell. Tossing the keys into the air and catching them, whistling a happy tune as he strolled back to his newly acquired Jaguar! Murmuring to himself as he walked,

"Well he was an old man anyway!"

The occurrence hardly if at all disturbed the tranquillity of this early morning idyll, the birds sang while the sun was yet to reach its zenith! It was ironic really, after all Albert had been warned by his doctor to stop this early morning session because of an irregular heartbeat, even his wife was very concerned about his insistence to carry on running. Strange how small problems have a way of solving themselves.

CHAPTER 3
The Unfortunates of Life!

I stood in my garden a lonely man, for death and time are such cruel masters. The violence I experienced in prison as also at other times in my life, always made me feel inwardly the same way as now, mind you—not to quite the same depth of feeling; but a long way towards it.

Experiencing that after the battle moment, even though maybe you're victorious, for me it always provokes a lonely feeling, embracing your mind and body; well—my senses are now reeling, not from victory but from defeat. Death reaching to grasp me fully and wholly in it's cold embrace, not as it's victim but holding me firmly as if in a vice; spiritually coercing me to be a hapless witness to all its triumphal cruel success.

Now when I think about the first catastrophe in my life, the accusations with final imprisonment for supposedly the murder of my colleague; that I knew was a complete fabrication of lies. Slander that cost me my job my future and almost my marriage. It was only with the faith of my parents back home in America; that helped me through this dark period in my life!

This was the episode that wiped away my life's good clean record, washing it away as if by a tsunami tide; a major incursion into my life which still hovers over me, I really did think at the time it was the end of the world, but in comparison to the loss of my wife, the threat to my life and well being; caused my personal world only to become ragged around the edges.

The important bit was we, that is, my wife and I—were both on this planet alive and kicking. I mean when you're alive you can handle almost anything, but when your dead, it really is the end, that is it! No come back tomorrow this is only a practice run; and as my cockney friends in prison would have said, you are brown bread—bloody dead once and for all.

Well she's buried now—her body certainly is, but not her memory, the pain I have felt from the start is still there; I suppose it always will be. The funeral—

it was terrible, having to cope with all the slings and arrows from her family, as if it was not enough to cope with just losing her.

They showed no pity, they all adopted the same attitude, carried the same arsehole faces; not once showing any sympathy towards me. At one point I wondered if they had all been to the same surgeon to receive special treatment, or lessons to achieve the same high quality distasteful expressions.

The discomfort they all planned to inflict, had no effect, their pathetic cruel reasoning went over my head; only grief swamped my body like a cold shower washing away their petty belligerence.

My latent thoughts happily transferred to the letter I received this morning from a very good friend. This friendship was forged by the hardship of prison life; I was stunned when I received the letter. It was unbelievable the timing of such a communication, as if God himself knew at this time I needed a friend.

Well providence took away my wife, my two young children were sent to boarding school, well—yes I needed a friend. The children, how awful it was to see them off, accompanied by their grandparents going to their new boarding school, it was just endless pain; I thanked God for the sunny day enabling me to escape from the house to my garden.

I sat down on the garden seat wondering, if it was time for me to consider seriously the offer which came in the letter from my very good friend Chip. While the whole plan was yet to unfold, I guessed it would be a bit of an adventure; he'd asked me to meet him in a café.

This particular cafe we used regularly when we were released from prison, in that extraordinary lonely margin of time before my wife finally took me back, for like most of my friends she was unbelievably unsure of my innocence; the whole world thought I was guilty—when I knew I was innocent.

I found the thought of the café still being there surprising, because I suppose that part of my life had vanished into the past; pushed and packed into the back of my mind as you would stamp unwanted personal articles into a dust bin. So— I expected in my mind the café to go the same way; but of course it hadn't!

I sat in the half empty café at three-o-clock in the afternoon, virtually nothing had changed, all the walls still needed a fresh lick of paint. I was sure that the old girl Nina, who was serving, was still holding the same fag in her mouth; nurturing an incredible length of ash, still wearing a forties style turban on her head. Nina remembered me—with a smile plus a sexy wink she muttered,

"You couldn't stay way from the old place then?"

I smiled, telling her I was only here to see her, she smiled back a big warm smile; raising her eyebrows, rolling her eyes in flattered exaggeration. I sat at the table near the window watching the heavy rainfall, what a difference to yesterday, still that's how it is. A tall character dressed in a black leather jacket with black trousers was running across the road, eager to get into the café out of the rain, it was my good friend Chip.

The émigré from the rain cloud, eagerly entered the café in the same way he'd came back into my life—suddenly. My good friend spotted me instantly sitting at the table by the window, he was bursting with alacrity, Chip took a big fresh white handkerchief from his pocket then proceeded to wipe his face dry with his left hand; while enthusiastically extended his right hand to shake mine. At the same time he wore a big happy grin across his swarthy handsome features; he spoke as he shook my hand, stuffing the handkerchief into his pocket, then pulling out a chair to sit at my table with his left hand,

"How are you old friend? I'm so pleased you came, I hoped your wife wouldn't stop you."

At this point he held out both hands indicating for me to pause, while he shouted to the lady behind the counter,

"Nina—a cup of tea for a drowned man please!"

The old girl nodded subtly, again without any change of expression on her face, I hesitated to tell him about my problems; it seemed a shame to spoil such a congenial reunion. Chip was as I remembered him, tall slim, about six four with a dash of Italian running through his veins, moulding his handsome features.

"Well Mister Garth Pilgrim our man from America, the terror of the third landing in that bloody prison; how are you? It's good to be with you, it makes a change not to be mixing with dwarfs." I replied,

"Being the terror of the third landing was thrust upon me; you never forget anything do you."

He was of course referring to the fighting with fellow criminals who hated policeman, Chip smiled answering,

"Not the important things anyway, I've got a deal offered me; I'd like you to join me. We have to find somebody for this crazy geezer—well he's a weirdo, but I think a harmless one. Money up front plenty of expenses, in fact a real cool deal. That is all I know about it, I want you with me—but I also used this as an excuse to see an old friend again, on top of that you're a good guy to have around. Especially when there is competition around; it seems to light up your inner self!" I laughed as I answered,

"You're still the impetuous fool of old Chip, is that all you know about the offer. Who is it we have to find? Why ask you? Why not the Police or private investigators?"

Chip shrugged his shoulders as he spoke,

"Pilgrim—the guy hates the police, he has already tried two private eyes that have proved to be useless; so he phoned me out of the blue a week ago. The gent advised me to get a partner, I wasn't doing anything—the bread sounded good—I thought of you, so here we are. He or one of his hirelings is supposed to be picking us up from here, I hope I get the chance to eat first, I'm starving."

I rubbed my chin thinking deeply about the words that had just been thrown at me.

"So you know no more than that Chip?"

I paused to think again. Chip butted in on my thoughts, blurting out a few sentences urging me to join him; like bullets from a gun.

"So are you coming to hear the rest of it? We can make our minds up then, come on lets give it a go, what have we got to lose?"

I laughed again,

"Okay I'll swing along with it, just to see what it's all about, then I'll make my mind up."

Chip pulled at the sleeve of my shirt as he spoke,

"That's the spirit; I told Julie you wouldn't let me down."

With the word "Julie" unknowingly to Chip all other images came swarming into my mind, a very pretty blonde girl whose figure would definitely launch a thousand ships, anyway she'd launch mine that's for certain; the fact I was married always kept me away from her. Now with recent events I'd still like to keep her a way from me—for a while anyway, I think the loss of my wife ought to be kept a secret until this intolerable ache decides to leave me—if ever it does, I couldn't help enquiring after Julie's well being,

"How's Julie?"

Chip smiled as he answered,

"Oh the same as ever, carrying a torch for you as she always did, it goes without saying she sends her regards."

I nodded smiling, perhaps I felt now as I did when I was in prison, captured by my own inhibitions—imprisoned by my own guilt. Why do I feel so guilty? There was nothing I could do about my wife's cancer! How on earth people say they are in charge of their own lives is beyond me, when we are all victims of circumstances.

"Pilgrim, Pilgrim! Can you hear me?"

I looked up at Chip in surprise,

"Of course I can, I was thinking about what you just said."

I lied to cover up my continual mental escape from reality; I knew I would have to tell Chip about my wife.

"Thinking!" Chip exclaimed in a loud voice.

"I thought you were daydreaming, what I was saying is when this guy takes us to see the man, I'd like you to say nothing, let me do all the talking." I nodded smiling while I added,

"My pleasure."

We hardly spoke while we ate, Chip finished his meal first pushing his plate away to the side, then ordered another two teas, he lit up a cigarette then stared at me long and hard before speaking to me again. That stare told me he knew there was something wrong,

"Come on then tell me all about it, what sort of trouble are you in? I might be able to solve it for you, I'm a good fixer."

I scooped up the last of the beans on my plate then placing my knife and fork together, pushed the empty dish away.

"I wish you could fix this for me, but I'm afraid you can't, it cannot be fixed."

Chip went to speak again, so I held my hand up indicating for him not to make another comment,

"My wife has just died from the big C, dead and buried, so now you know. It is what it is—please don't say you're sorry, because all the sympathy in the world won't make any difference. You are a life saver offering me this work, taking me away from that bloody house and that area with all the middle class snobs where I live; who sneer at me every time they see me, knowing I have just come out of jail! That is it, I can't say much more because there's nothing more too say."

Chip just sat there looking at his old friend beginning to feel his grief, unsure where to start or even too start, or maybe change the subject; but decided to go for the throat.

"Do you want to talk about it?"

I shook my head,

"No—I don't but thanks anyway."

Chip drew in a deep breath answering,

"Okay that's fine, one thing's for sure we're going to be busy so don't keep drifting off into the past, I need you now here with me."

I smiled answering,

"I also *need* to be here with you Chip old friend."

There was a loud blast from a car horn as I finished the last sentence, the noise drew our eyes to the origin of the noisemaker as we glanced through the window, Chip recognised the driver of a large new shiny black Mercedes and waved to him, then quickly turned to say, "It's the man, come on let's go!"

CHAPTER 4
So You Have Sampled My Sister's Talents!

M oses Dolan knew this area well; it was where he first came to when he left north Yorkshire in a hurry, to avoid the tentacles of M I 5. Paddington was after all, right under the noses of the arrogant pigs (Police); this particular drinking club in the basement of a run down property used to be one of his favourite haunts.

The club was run by a very large coloured man called Kevan, he surrounded himself with several coloured men of the same stature; these particular characters always made a fuss of Moses. They admired him for being what he was, anything or anybody who made a stand against authority, drew not only their admiration but their undying loyalty!

Moses glanced at his watch as he went down the steps to the basement door of the club, the time was two thirty. The appointment was for three o clock in the afternoon, it was several months since he was last here; although he thought it a good idea to arrive early to rekindle old acquaintances, in case a little added physical protection was needed.

The people he was going to meet, originally employed him to acquire the package, the killing of the old man at the sports ground had presented no problems, in fact it was all too easy. As for the person who employed him to do the killing, Moses decided an extra degree of negotiations wouldn't do any harm to try and up the fee; realising they would not be very pleased to hear such a suggestion!

The assassin's blonde hair good looks orchestrated by a voice with the added friendly northern accent with charming ways, belied the ruthless streak that lay under the veneered charisma! He made his way to the bar surveying his surroundings, he also studied furtively the other occupants of the little club then ordered a drink. He greeted the barman like an old friend, and then sat himself down on a stool to wait for these "bloody weirdo's" to appear, as he called them.

The bar was still the same—in need of a coat of paint, the walls still hung with out dated yellowing exotic posters of the Caribbean, matching the off white painted walls that partnered the musty smell, but the alcohol was cheap. It most likely fell off the back of a lorry—as they say.

One of his old friends and assistants to the owner waved to him from the other side of the dimly lit bar, which pleased him. Mo as he was called by all his former associates didn't have to wait long for his employer to enter with four of his henchman. They saw him instantly, pointing to the corner of the bar for him to join them, but never spoke a word.

Moses threw back his double whisky then moved to join the group in a poorly lit corner. The man who employed him was an ugly bastard; there is no other way of putting it. On his shoulders he carried a large bulbous head with a stuck on long pointed thin nose, decorated by a profuse of warts also covering his forehead, balanced off with two ears that stuck out like leaves from a wrinkled cabbage. Matching his thin straight straggly strands of hair, hanging down his back like an unemployed November the fifth Guy! His name was Harrison; Moses always thought it should have been Fawkes!

The other four men were just hired thugs, which anybody could pick up if they were willing to shell out a good few pretty shillings.

As Moses sat down he felt an assuring dig from his piece, which was stuck down the front of his trousers, ready to blow all five of these bastards into an early grave—if he has to. The barman hurriedly placed a drink in front of each man who now sat with Moses; while Harrison spoke with a hoarse cultured accent.

"Now listen carefully to me! You were paid to do a job for me, to bring a particular object with you to this meeting; I know you've done the job; you have also collected the article. Suddenly we receive from you a garbled telephone call, that you want more money than the agreed sum. The person who recommended you assured me of your reliability, I don't expect this sort of treachery from people I employ!"

Moses remained silent for a moment before answering, just staring at the demanding interrogator exuding pure arrogance, when he did speak he did so with great clarity and emphasis,

"The garbled phone call you received was from me, asking for more money for the article I have in my possession, it's simple, I want more money! Whatever you do, please don't threaten me with these old farts, because the article in question is hidden away. If anything happens to me, it will never be found again."

One of the old farts Moses referred to was an elderly gentleman smartly dressed like a city gent, who had escaped from his office for a few hours. The elderly epigone leant forward speaking very quietly to Moses,

"I know you have a sister who plies her wares in Soho. I must admit she is very good at what she does, performs a very good blow job. I hope nothing happens to her, she's such a nice girl."

These remarks caused Moses to smile as he again spoke slowly and emphatically,

"Oh, you have sampled her hospitality and now you are threatening her life, well just remember if anything happens to her or me; you will never find the article you are seeking in a hundred years! So why don't you just pay the money, so that you can have what you want instantly."

Harrison grimaced as he said,

"The amount you asked for was a clear one million pounds, deposited into a bank outside the UK; is that correct?"

Moses nodded as he answered,

"Yes that's correct, I'm sure that's mere chicken feed to the likes of a powerful man like you."

The man with the bulbous head, with a big nose covered with warts accompanied by big ears leant over the table—to speak in a very soft tone of voice,

"I'm beginning to forget all about the bloody article I sent you for, because you're making me very angry; I hate to get like this, but you leave me no alternative. So I'll put it to you, if I don't hear from you in ten days I will kill your sister then you, do I make myself clear."

The ugly bastard sat back to watch the face of the young assassin, to study the impact of his statements. Unfortunately for Harrison, Moses was a good poker player, quite used to playing in games with higher stakes than this. So nothing showed in his face; which did not please the bulbous headed ugly man. In fact the blonde headed man pushed back his chair from the table then burst out laughing; before answering in his rich Yorkshire accent,

"Does thou really think thee can kill me with these candidates from dad's army, sweet Jesus? I'll say this about you, you're a bloody optimist."

The ugly man stood up in a rage motioning his henchman to follow him pausing for one second to repeat his threat,

"Remember you have ten days to fulfil my request otherwise you are a dead man."

Moses watched them go as he muttered with a half smile on his face,
"You'll pay the money, or I will kill you—and that's a promise Mister ugly bastard!"

CHAPTER 5
Find the Assassin!

They must have been travelling for an hour before Chip spoke, "I thought you were only taking us to Mayfair not bloody Scotland? The character driving who looked like Al Capone's minder, answered in a hoarse south London accent as heavy smokers do.

"The man you are going to see is my boss Tobias Friedman, he has just bought a big place in Grantham, and he was caught up in a meeting with several business associates, so he decided to bring you both there to stay for a few days. You'll like the place it used to be occupied by a bunch of Jesuit priests, it stood empty for about ten years until the boss bought it; it's as creepy as hell—you'll find out."

Pilgrim asked,

"How much further have we to go?"

"Not far, not far." Muttered the driver.

So Pilgrim dozed off, he didn't know how long for—but awoke as they were going down a long drive about a mile long which was poorly lit; the building was visible from a distance, what the driver said about it being creepy was exactly right.

The architecture was very ugly, it had onion domes with heavy stone mouldings capped by tall misshapen Victoriana brick chimneys, shrouded in a drifting mist, assisted by the failing light creating lengthening shadows, producing a sort of Dracula film aura. Chip had also fallen asleep, yet like Pilgrim had woken as they were in the drive approaching the house.

"You weren't lying when you said it was creepy, how did he manage to find this place?"

The driver shrugged his shoulders as he spoke,

"I really don't know, he's a weirdo anyway, but he pays good money to people who don't mind what they do, so here I am."

The car stopped at the front entrance; a row of stone steps covered by an ornate stone Victorian portico. The driver stepped out of the car, so did Chip with Pilgrim, then they both stood staring at this large gargantuan eighteen century conception wondering what was in store for them. They looked at each other then climbed the steps together; the front door was being opened by an unseen hand which was gradually spilling out a soft yellow light illuminating the drifting mist; as they approached it.

The door opened out into exactly what was expected, a specimen of splendid Victorian architectural design at its best—beauty at its ugliest. A marble staircase bordered with an ornately carved flowing handrail supported with heavily enriched balustrade, winding up three floors.

At the moment one could only see it flowing into the consuming darkness of the upper area, with heavily ornamental ceilings adorned in gold and white, the walls panelled with the same gold painted mouldings reaching up to the gold leaf enriched cornice.

The two visitors stood for a moment while the driver motioned for them to follow the butler; who spoke in a well-cultured voice; but he also had the natural appearance of a man who knew exactly what was expected of him and did exactly that. The butler's appearance was just about acceptable with his arrogant manner, but Chip and Pilgrim still felt very ill at ease with the environmental ambience and the butler, also of course the person who had encouraged them to follow him. While he radiated all the characteristics of a butler, they felt he more than likely had a gun tucked up his sleeve to go with his wide shoulders and flat nose.

Chip along with Pilgrim were ushered into a large room, what the upper class would call a drawing room, opulently furnished in the best tastes of the same era of the rest of the house, pursuing that same unsettling atmosphere.

Both men stood for a while surveying their surroundings, before sitting down in large armchairs opposite each other, wondering what or who was coming next; it wasn't long before their curiosity was satisfied. The door opened to reveal a bespectacled man in a wheelchair, aged about fifty, greying hair bright cold blue eyes set in sallow gaunt features.

He was pushed into the room by our old friend the flat nosed butler, he remained behind the wheelchair tacitly unmoving; his face expressionless. The man in the wheelchair smiled an attempted smile, as if frightened to give away too much even a welcoming grin, as he spoke.

"Thank you for coming, my name is Tobias Friedman, I've looked forward to your appearance; a little concerned as to whether or not you would keep our appointment. I thought perhaps my offer to you Chip was a little unclear, but now you're here I will clarify the situation or should I say the terms of employment; while I realise you have had an unexpected journey. I will not waste time on the veneer of introductory formalities, but hasten to clarify the duties I want you to fulfil.

All my life I've searched for the golden chalice; unfortunately I'm not alone in this pursuit. Several weeks ago I came very near to acquiring this artefact but it was stolen from the man who was delivering it to me, unfortunately my enemies murdered him; so the exact whereabouts of the object is now unknown.

I have some names with a few addresses, which will assist you in your inquiries. Money is no problem, only one important factor is paramount, I want this jewel of life in my hand; I will provide you with all your needs and more. Although I must warn you this venture is highly dangerous, it could cost you your lives." Just for those fleeting seconds the man in the wheelchair stopped for what seemed a theatrical pause, then resumed to study closely the faces that were receiving this information, choosing his words slowly—with care!

"If you feel this is too much for you, please don't hesitate to tell me. For once you are committed there is no turning back, pulling out from the deal unfinished; will without doubt definitely cost you your lives."

Here the wheelchair man paused again to study their reactions, momentarily searching for any change of facial expressions, but he received no response from the stone like features, so he resumed to orally exhibit a show of sincerity with further promises of large bounties to be earned.

"A meal has been prepared for you with a comfortable bed for the night, also every personal accessory you require, toothbrushes along with new night attire all in your rooms. In the morning, I will want to know the answer; the monetary reward for success will be very high."

"This will be of great interest to you, I offer riches gentlemen, of course it's high risk with real adventure. What you must both decide, are you man enough for the task? I look forward to discussing it with you again first thing in the morning, think very carefully about this, before you make the decision either way. So I will bid you good night gentlemen."

The wheel chaired occupant disappeared through the double doors pushed by his loyal butler as quickly as he appeared, leaving Chip and Pilgrim to dwell on what the spectacled invalid offered.

"What do you think?"

Asked Chip, Pilgrim looked at Chip shrugging his shoulders as he answered,

"I thought we were in this just to find a missing person, now it seems we are about to participate in a highly dangerous mission which would be better suited to an SAS team; then you ask me what do I think! I really don't know, but I must admit the large amounts of money he mentions sounds good."

Chip smiled then shook his head.

"Well I must say I agree with you."

The entrance of the flat nosed butler closed the conversation,

"Gentlemen will you please follow me, then I will show you to your rooms, where your meal will be served."

Old flat nose turned and made his way out of the room towards the ornate staircase, which greeted them on their entrance to the house. They followed unspoken in a silent procession plodding up the stairs, then along the corridors, until the butler intimated with his finger; that they had reached the first room for one of them to enter.

Pilgrim nodded to Chip; Chip smiled as he then stepped inside, while Pilgrim marched on in silence; following the guide to the room next door. He grunted, Pilgrim nodded in cooperation, then he also opened the door to step inside, closed the door, waited for the footsteps to fade away down the corridor then reopened the door, to make his way back to Chip's room.

Chip was sitting on his bed obviously waiting for his friend to return. As he walked into the room the bedside phone rang, Chip hesitated then picked it up, answering,

"Hello."

He listened for a moment before answering again,

"Thank you that would do very nicely also I'm sure my colleague would also be grateful for a cup of tea!!"

Chip then put the phone down then looked at Pilgrim to say,

"We've got some tea coming, they've set a table over there for us to eat our dinner; how does that suit you?"

Pilgrim nodded answering.

"That's just fine I am very hungry."

The two men sat at the table set for dinner, eager to discuss the finer points of the earlier conversation.

"Chip what is this golden chalice that he spoke about, they're talking about it as if it's worth killing for and also expect to be killed, what the hell is it?"

It was Chip's turn to shrug his shoulders,

"I'm not sure but I was always led to believe it was the chalice Jesus drank his wine from during the last supper!"

Pilgrim never answered for several minutes thinking about the Grail, something that he would in normal circumstances stand in fear of, but now,

"The surprising point is Pilgrim, is him asking us to think about it, then give him a decision in the morning; think about what? We haven't a clue what it's all about never mind making our mind's up!"

"How did you meet this guy, who is he? Even the man who drove us up here said he was a weirdo, so how the hell did you meet him?"

Chip never answered right away but hesitated to think about the answer,

"I have never met the man before in my life, I was recommended by an independent party; in actual fact—a very good friend of mine. He introduced me to this man Tobias over the phone."

Pilgrim took a deep breathe then expelled the air from his lungs in exasperation,

"Chip this gets better all the time, by the way you spoke in the café I took it for granted that this guy was an old friend!"

Chip rolled his eyes as he answered.

"Now you know different, anyway this type of chatter is going nowhere, the point is—are we going to say yes or no to this guy?"

"Chip let's sleep on it, because I think we still have plenty of questions to ask before we make a decision."

The knock on the door brought the conversation to an abrupt halt. Chip called out,

"Come in!"

Another individual whom they had never seen before entered the room with two cups of tea, he placed them carefully on the table; he then cleared away the empty plates leaving the room without saying a single word. Chip folded his arms across his chest then dropped his gaze to the floor as he spoke,

"Pilgrim I agree with you, so yes let's sleep on it."

His good friend nodded in agreement then said,

"Right we'll do just that."

He turned to go as Chip called out to him,

"Don't forget your tea!"

Pilgrim stopped then answered over his shoulder in a loud voice,

"You drink it; it's too late at night for me to drink tea."

Pilgrim was tired the bed was very comfortable; the room was as good as any first class hotel with its en suite facilities with the secondary lighting taking the room into semi darkness, giving him time to think as he lay in the half light.

Pilgrim's mind started running through the chain of events over the last few unforgettable months, suddenly Pilgrim was sure he could hear a murmur of voices; at first he thought it was pure imagination. But when he really concentrated on listening intently, yes he definitely could hear voices; Pilgrim stepped slowly out of the bed to see if he could trace exactly where the sounds were coming from.

His ears led him to a cupboard by the side of the bed, he came to the conclusion that this cupboard must have been acting like a sound carrier from downstairs. The voices now were very clear, Pilgrim stood motionless; absorbing every word committing them to memory. A gruff voice spoke,

"What did the governor think of the two guys upstairs?"

Pilgrim recognised the voice of old flat nose but didn't know the owners of the other two voices.

"He didn't say a lot, but I think they'll take it on, they look a couple of mugs."

A third voice spoke that Pilgrim didn't recognise,

"They must be, to be here in the first place."

Then it was the butler's turn to answer,

"I don't think they're a couple of mugs, I reckon they will definitely take the job on, I suppose then we are going to have the job of tracking them. I don't think it's going to be an easy task."

Old flat nose spoke,

"I hope they do, let's face it we are talking about a lot of money, so to get it; means they will in the end get knocked off."

The second voice spoke,

"Keep your voices down, the sound carries in this old place."

The voice of the flat nosed butler answered,

"It can carry all it likes they won't hear it, I doped their tea. I'll bet they're sleeping like babies! That one they call Pilgrim, is a joke he was fitted up by one of the men he used to work with, receiving five years. He was lucky enough to have a murder charge dropped to manslaughter, but got discharged after two; so he can't be all that bright. They will not live very long against the villains they're going to meet!"

These shocking revelations concerning the tea along with the comments on Pilgrim's personal life really made him feel vulnerable and very angry! So pulling on his trousers, Pilgrim crept out of the room to knock gently on Chip's door, there was no answer.

So he let himself in, moving quickly over to the bedside to see Chip laying there on his back snoring heavily. Pilgrim shook Chip roughly but not a movement came from him, a glance told him that the two teacups were empty; this explained why he was in such a deep sleep.

Sitting on the edge of the bed Pilgrim pondered the facts not understanding why anybody would go to all the trouble to do this for no reason, it just made no sense. Obviously they were frightened of Chip and Pilgrim doing, or worse still seeing something very unsavoury that we would not like, it was all a mystery. Hell! Pilgrim wished Chip hadn't touched the bloody tea. For Pilgrim thought it was time he went exploring, it would have been good to have Chip for company.

He was very nervous, overhearing the thug's remarks made him realise the danger they were in, as well as being unarmed. Pilgrim sneaked out making his way to the top of the house ignoring the creepy half shadows, where your instincts tells you someone is hiding but never is. Carefully and very quietly, systematically trying all the doors then looking into the rooms where the doors opened.

This particular room that he found was very strange, it was more like a hall in fact it definitely had the feel of a temple, it was very large; the floor was laid out in diagonal black and white tiles. In the centre of the floor red tiles were laid in the shape of a pentacle.

At the far end of this room was an ornately carved legged table with a white veined black marble top, next to it an effigy of a haired human figure, with a goat's head sitting cross legged in an ornamental carver chair; with its arms and clawed hands placed comfortably along the arms of the seat.

The walls were covered in dark oak wooden panelling; at appointed intervals were decorated with heavily detailed carved wooden grotesque satanic gargoyles. There was a six foot diameter domed circular small paned glass window directly above the pentacle, with a circular lighting trough running around underneath it; emitting a soft light, casting half shadows over the Victoriana architecture and all the adorning snarling gargoyles imposing a ghost like threatening presence.

At the opposite end of the room hung a set of chained linked metal bracelets, as Pilgrim moved closer even in the poor light he could see the blood stains on the wall and floor. The stale scent of incense along with the Devil's aura of the temple caused shudders to ripple down his spine, standing there alone in the gloom of semi darkness; Pilgrim wondered what evil prevailed in this house. He turned and left this place, thinking this was the

Devil's abode; feeling a lot happier when the door closed, then he moved on down the corridor to see what else could be found.

After that the next half dozen rooms were empty but the seventh room showed signs of life, the bed was unmade the wardrobe door was open. Pilgrim moved further into the room, his eyes flitting around the area trying to take in every detail.

The room was operating on the secondary lighting as in his own room when the bathroom door opened, suddenly a tall dark figure entered, when he saw Pilgrim he froze unmoving. The tall dark haired stranger blurted out a question in a fearful manner,

"What do you want here? There is nothing here for you, I've already told them all I know and I've nothing to add."

The voice was a cultured Scottish voice; the accent was from Edinburgh, a striking contrast to those thugs Pilgrim had just been listening to. He moved a little closer—Pilgrim could see he was a man about fifty-five, dark curly hair chubby faced quite tall and well dressed.

Pilgrim's mind was now in turmoil, racing trying to think, wanting to know what this man was doing here, and why the anxious tone in his voice. Was it fear? Was he being held here against his will? Pilgrim spoke slowly picking his words carefully.

"I'm not exactly with the other guys here, more trying to find out why I'm here, perhaps you can help me?"

A very worried look came over the man's face,

"I don't understand what you say, you mean you're not with these other men, are you here to threaten me, what do you want?"

Pilgrim moved a bit closer to the bed then sat on it, thinking that this action might calm him down; the last thing he wanted was for this concerned looking character to start shouting his head off; so Pilgrim spoke to him in a soft friendly voice.

"Look I don't know who you are, actually I don't care, I would just like answers to a few questions, I have no reason to hurt you in any way."

The stranger stroked his chin while staring at Pilgrim; he then spoke after several seconds passed,

"You really don't know anything do you."

He also sat down on the bed next to Pilgrim as he spoke,

"I think you are caught up in something you ought not to be."

Pilgrim was now getting a little irritable and impatient with all this secrecy,

"So you know the answers to all this?"

The older man heaved a sigh casting his eyes around the room in a display of despair, "I was invited here on the pretence that I was an expert in the field of holy artefacts, unfortunately after being here for a short while it soon became obvious that it really was a different agenda. You see they are aware I know the whereabouts of—"

The noise of someone running up the corridor caused the man to stop speaking, but then add hastily;

"Please I beg of you go for your own safety and mine, go through this door to the next room and leave that way; they're bound to come in here first, please go quickly!"

This quiet spoken man was now frightened because he wanted Pilgrim out of his space; Pilgrim still did not know what all the fuss was about. So he ran to the adjacent room as the character suggested, waited for the thugs to burst into where he'd just left. Then, Pilgrim ran out of the door through the corridor down the stairs back into Chips room, one glance told him Chip was still dead to the world.

Standing next to Chip's bed made Pilgrim feel vulnerable, he knew he would have to stay with him to stand guard. So he pulled a carver chair over to a dark corner of the room deciding to wait it out there, to at least until dawn broke; hopefully Chip would be awake by then.

Pilgrim sat listening for any movement from the thugs but heard nothing, then tried to stay awake for as long as possible, but in the end succumbed to the dark cloak of sleep.

Pilgrim's beloved wife came walking into his dreams, how beautiful she looked, it was once again the summer days of when they were younger; surrounded and enthralled by the promises of future happiness. How tantalisingly close she was, yet how far when he tried to hold her tightly in his arms. Still they laughed and ran and ran through the grass until she was out of sight— nowhere to be found.

Pilgrim awakened to find himself showered by the morning sun, bursting through the adjacent window while he was hanging over the side of the chair; staring at the carpet. For a few moments Pilgrim just couldn't work out where he was, suddenly it all came back. Pulling himself upright in the chair, he started running through his mind all the events of the previous night; which still made no sense!

Chip's eyes suddenly flicked open, his mind struggling to find its way through the cobwebs of heavy sleep. His observing guard knew exactly what the problem was going to be; waiting for the words to flow from his mouth and they did,

"What the hell happened to me last night? What are you doing sitting there?"

Pilgrim spent the following half an hour explaining to Chip what actually had occurred while he was in an induced sleep. Chip was angry over being drugged, but nevertheless fascinated by the description of the temple like room, which Pilgrim stumbled upon, yet more than concerned about the remarks of Pilgrim being fitted up by fellow M I 6 colleagues!

"Do you think we're mixed up with some sort of black magic?" Pilgrim laughed at Chip's naive question then answered,

"I am certain of that, for sure it's something evil; tell me Chip do you believe in God?"

"Of course I do, especially with what I've witnessed in the drug squad makes you aware of the evil people in life, there has to be a God to control them."

"The point is Chip are these thugs working for this Tobias Friedman? Or are they in it for their own ends? At this time there is no way we can find out. I also am starting to worry about our contractual relationship, if and when we manage to succeed in finding this man, will we then be able to walk away freely without any further aggravation?"

Chip rubbed his chin as he answered,

"I would like to know that as well, so we'll ask when we meet him at breakfast."

It was Pilgrim's turn to nod as he answered,

"Okay, come on let's get ready."

Pilgrim went back to his own room, both men showered and shaved with the toiletries provided, then eagerly made their way down to breakfast; their urgency partly fuelled by curiosity but also by hunger! The flat nosed thug masquerading in the butler's uniform stood waiting out of sight for them to settle at the table, before appearing to take their orders for breakfast.

Both men sat waiting for food like two well behaved school boys, ate their fill, then as the dirty plates were being removed by the butler Chip nodded to his friend—Pilgrim acknowledged with a nod back—then made the inquiry,

"Excuse me are we going to see Tobias this morning?

He did say he expected a decision from us this morning."

The butler never hesitated for one moment, he answered without even thinking about it.

"He will be here in due course."

The pugnacious looking butler took the last of the plates placing them at the end of the table, then the butler disappeared; we thought to fetch the character in the wheel chair.

"What do you think Pilgrim?"

Pilgrim smiled at Chip's impatience, but never answered. Before Pilgrim could think of a suitable answer the door opened, revealing the employer in the wheel chair; his entrance ably assisted by the butler. He sat for a moment pausing before he spoke, an exact hesitation that smacked of the theatrical, then he spoke quietly slowly but very clearly,

"Well gentlemen, have you an answer? Are you interested in working for me?"

Both men sat for a moment in silence actually not knowing what to say, Chip broke the silence,

"When we work for people we like to know what we are doing, at the moment we are wondering if we are just being taken for a couple of fools!"

Tobias again used the theatrical pause before he answered.

"Young man—I can't stop anybody thinking what they want to think, that is their business, all I'm asking you to do, is find someone for me, when you do— notify me immediately. For that small effort I'm willing to pay a bonus of half a million pounds each, with expenses up front of ten thousand pounds apiece. Now young man if that's being taken for a fool; then I wish someone would treat me like one!"

This very smooth answer from this person in the wheelchair, reflected completely a clever brain that for the moment disarmed both of them,

Pilgrim was stunned he quickly glanced sideways at Chip; for he was lost for words but soon collected his senses.

"How can you possibly offer us that sort of money when you know nothing about us?"

The elderly man smiled shaking his head,

"Do you think for one moment in time I would throw that sort of money around if I knew nothing about you? I happen to be a very wealthy man, in fact a rich man with a dream. What that dream is—" Here the bespectacled rich character in the wheelchair hesitated before resuming; obviously not wanting to tell us too much about himself or his protracted dreams,

"I didn't get rich by not knowing who I'm dealing with, I know your complete history from the day you were born Pilgrim, which was in America; English mother an American father. You served three years with the American Rangers, becoming attracted to England because of your parentage to join the English Parachute regiment, and then the SAS; you left the services to become an M I 6 agent. Someone, you don't know who, fitted you up with enough evidence to prove you killed your M I 6 colleague Tregear, even so you were lucky for the charge to be changed to manslaughter, then was fortunate to be discharged after two years.

That's where you met your friend here, who is an ex copper who also spent time in prison for falling in love with a prostitute, an act which eventually ruined his life. The important bit is you are both conversant with the criminals of the underworld! Do I need to go on? Oh one more important detail, you love your America but also love living here in the UK."

Pilgrim could not believe his ears, this old fool sitting in front of them was not an old fool at all. He looked across at Chip as Chip started to speak,

"You make it sound so easy that you know so much about us, why the hell do you need us to find this person?"

The invalid drew in a deep breath before he answered the question,

"The answer to that is simple; the people I'm looking for aren't as honest as you two. They are habitually violent and will kill you if they have to without blinking an eyelid, then disappear into the underworld. I'm sure I've found a good combination, I also think you both have the trained ability to handle this situation; but have you the courage?"

Chip looked over to his friend asking,

"Shall we take it?"

Pilgrim looked at Chip answering decisively,

"Bloody right we'll take it."

Tobias smiled the cat's smile when it had at last managed to acquire the stolen cream! Then he carried on speaking slowly—with heavy emphasis,

"I will leave you now gentleman, we've agreed our financial arrangements, you will be given your expenses before you leave.

When you return to your respective bedrooms you will each find a brown envelope, inside the envelope are your instructions with the necessary information, along with essential photographs; understand them, learn them, then destroy them. One other thing I want you to

leave at night fall, it will be to your advantage; I don't want you killed before you have had time to spend some of your expenses."

Tobias gave the order to his butler to take him away, but just as the chair was being turned he remembered something else, holding up his fore finger to the butler as a signal to stop for a moment.

"Oh I was sorry to hear about your wife Garth, please listen to an old fool. Try not to think too much about the past only the future, that way you short-circuit the pain. Also there was our friend you met, when you went looking around last night, please don't worry about him he's quite safe. I would like you to know Pilgrim I am aware that you are totally innocent of those charges that were brought against you, never mind, as I have already said we mustn't brood on the past!"

Once again Tobias gave the order to his sycophantic butler to push him away. Before this could happen, Chip suddenly threw the question at the elderly man.

"Mr. Friedman what is the golden chalice?"

The enigmatic invalid who liked to be called Toby, turned his head quickly as if a nerve had just been touched, his eyes narrowing as he spoke the gratuitous smile dropping from his lips as he answered very sharply,

"You will have to learn that I'm like a game show host, only I ask the questions."

"That as may be Mister Friedman but there is one more question we would like to ask before you leave!"

Toby heaved an enormous sigh before he answered in a slow deliberate manner,

"Well gentlemen you'd better ask it—hadn't you."

Pilgrim cleared his throat before proceeding with the important question that they'd both discussed before coming down to breakfast.

"If and when we complete the task set before us, then as paid hirelings; will we be able to walk away with no further obligations or dangers to ourselves?"

Tobias Friedman sat for a moment that seemed like an hour before he answered,

"If you are successful in the task I have set you, then on completion you choose to walk away, there will be no problem attached to that decision."

Pilgrim shrugged his shoulders, casting a sidelong glance at Chip as he answered,

"Okay that's all we wanted to know."

The invalid departed, pushed by his loyal butler; leaving Chip with Pilgrim to wonder at the man's ability to know everything that happens around him. He remarked to Chip,

"I haven't been called Garth for many years."

Chip smiled,

"Oh yes that's an old mind game—to make you feel inferior, he's clever alright; we still don't know the answers do we?"

Pilgrim stared up at the ceiling for a moment before answering Chip, then his eyes dropped to look at Chip as he replied,

"I've no doubt the plot will unfold as we progress."

"Eh you! You've never told me you were in the Paras!" Chip smiled,

"I hate to say it but you never asked, and lets face it when we first met the last thing we were interested in was our past lives, besides that you never told me about the prostitute you were in love with, what about that. That sounds far more interesting than being in the Parachute regiment!"

"Man that old boy is clever, he's really got to us. Never mind no doubt we will learn more about each other as well, come on let's go and find our brown envelopes."

They made their way up to the rooms once again; there on the bedside tables as promised were the letters. Pilgrim picked his up then went into Chip's room they both sat on the bed opening their little presents, like schoolboys smiling and laughing as they did.

There was a cheque for each of them in separate envelopes for nine thousand pounds with one thousand pound in cash, the old readies as Chip liked to call it. Chip and Pilgrim both realised they were in this up to their necks, now they had accepted the King's shilling there was no going back; so come hell or high water they made up their minds; that they would not rest until the half a million bonus was in their pockets.

The young adventurers left at dusk, the dark shadows were now pulling in fast, accompanied by the swirling mists that greeted them on the evening of their arrival. Pilgrim turned around to get a last glimpse of the Victorian pile through the rear window, of the new series BMW with a number plate of 777 DEV, that Toby had arranged to be delivered for their personal use.

He turned away and wondered if they would live to regret ever seeing this antique pile of bricks and mortar. Chip broke his stare from the road in front of him to cast a sideways glance at Pilgrim as he spoke,

"What are you thinking about Pilgrim? You seem to have gone very quiet; you're not having second thoughts are you?"

Pilgrim smiled as he spoke,

"I was thinking about the future, until I met you in the café it was something that never existed, all I had was ferocious unsociable attitudes from neighbours and relations. Now I have something, it's a bit bloody thin but at least it's something. The thought keeps rushing into my mind; perhaps we will be lucky to stay alive. I have read the details of the character we are about to pursue, I have had great experience chasing the Patriotic British Party members; they are very ruthless and elusive."

Chip nodded as he answered,

"I understand what you're saying, please—read out to me the known history of the gangster we're tracking down."

Pilgrim took out the package from the glove compartment, carefully pulling out the typed record of the wanted man; then proceeded to read aloud the history from the document.

"MOSES DOLAN HAS AN ENGLISH MOTHER AND A GERMAN FATHER; HE IS AN EX "PATRIOTIC BRITISH PARTY" MEMBER, GENERALLY KNOWN AS THE PBP. A VERY DANGEROUS MAN, TOP OF THE SPECIAL BRANCH WANTED LIST. HE SERVED FIVE YEARS IN THE PARACHUTE REGIMENT, FOUR YEARS IN THE FRENCH FOREIGN LEGION, ALSO WANTED IN THREE OTHER COUNTRIES FOR THE ASSASSINATING OF LEADING POLITICAL LEADERS. AT THE MOMENT HE IS EMPLOYED AS AN INTERNATIONAL HIT MAN BY AN UNKNOWN PRIVATE CLIENT. YOUR MISSION IS TO CAPTURE THIS MAN AND TAKE HIM TO THE MANSION AT GRANTHAM. HE WAS LAST SEEN ON A TRAINING GROUND IN SURREY, LATER TRACKED TO A FLAT IN VICTORIA LONDON. YOU MUST REMEMBER THIS MAN IS AN ACCOMPLISHED KILLER. ALSO YOU WOULD DO WELL TO CALL IN TO SEE A PROSTITUTE CALLED TEREASA WHO IS HIS SISTER; BASED AT THE SOHO ADDRESS BELOW.

The reading was met by silence from both men, it started to rain so Chip turned on the wipers, the silence was then broken by the swish swash of the wiper blades.

"I understand why you feel the way you do, this is the same as when you were in the SAS tracking the Patriot's training ground location?" There was another silence before Pilgrim answered,

"Chip there is one difference; we were caught up in a straight jacket of rules related to the God democracy. Well you and I are not, so—we can stoop to the same filthy tricks as the clever man whom we are following, an individual which I consider to be a curse to this nation."

Chips face turned very serious as he cast another sideways glance at Pilgrim, strangely enough; Chip noted that Pilgrim's character within this straitjacket of danger was emerging as a sterner more serious type than before!

"I sense a note of bitterness in your voice."

"Don't worry Chip—I have first hand knowledge of our Patriotic Members. One fact keeps running through my mind, Tobias didn't want us leaving in daylight hours. Are we being watched at this time, if we are—we could be dead men walking? The point I'm making is, are we expected at this address we've been given! I think we ought to make for West London for at least two nights, then see what sort of action we create. Oh, what about the photograph? Do we keep it or destroy it along with the letter?"

Chip was quick to answer,

"I agree with everything you say Pilgrim, as for the picture I think we'll keep it. Where are we going to stay tonight?"

"As I said Chip, West London seems the place to go, it has a glut of boarding houses in that area; have you a preference? Of course we must both appreciate it's impossible to go anywhere near our homes or relations."

Chip thought for a moment then said,

"When I was with the flying squad we used several small hotels in West London, there's one around the corner from Olympia, and we always booked in; then paid for the night. But prior to booking in we would park our car three streets away, and then leave by the fire exit. It was to make sure there was no one following us; we could not allow ourselves to be found by the drug gangs."

"I understand Chip, but there's one point you also must comprehend, always remember we never sleep at the same time, if you sleep I must stay awake. Otherwise we will not live for very long."

Chip nodded as he answered,

"I absolutely agree, so first we'll make for the hotel to use the booking system I spoke about."

A moments silence fell upon them, but Chip could almost hear Pilgrim's mind working, sensing there was something churning through his mind; causing him to smile when Pilgrim did at last speak.

"There are a few words that keep running through my mind you know Chip, they keeps nagging at me all the time."

"What is it; it's not the kids at home is it?"

"Oh no I'm sure they are okay! It's just the cocksure way Tobias stated that he knew I was innocent! I just feel he must have the answer to my problems."

Pilgrim spoke slowly and emphatically as he finished the latter part of the sentence.

"But how could he possibly know?"

Chip never answered, he thought about it but mentally concluded—some questions are better not answered!

CHAPTER 6
She Must Have Been a Beautiful Baby!

The distinguished looking elderly character with black greying hair at his temples, accompanied by thin flaccid features with a pointed nose, was wearing a dark blue pinstriped suit with a white collared blue shirt; sporting a blue and maroon diagonally striped regimental Royal Artillery neck tie.

At first glance he looked a typical product of the old Victorian style middle class, sitting on the park bench his cold blue eyes seemed to be absorbing the contents of the Times newspaper. Now and then taking a bite from a sandwich, one of many in a fastidiously quartered package carefully unfolded then laid neatly by his side. His total attire blended with a bearing of arrogant stoic superiority; in fact he looked an absolute picture of snobbish respectability.

Although his smile was nearer a sneer, anybody sparing a second glance at the sartorially attired elderly gentlemen would never think the slight bulge in his left breast jacket pocket was a snub nosed Smith and Weston.

The weapon, along with his evil identity was hidden amongst the mannerisms of his portrayal of an honest hard working middle class office worker. He sat there enjoying the warm morning sun casually feeding the ducks with the odd pinch of bread, attracting a gathering of feathered friends from the calm waters of the lake to his feet.

This still didn't stop this despot from being seemingly totally engrossed in the business page, even when a very attractive young lady arrived to sit next to him. She also was dressed in a blue pinstriped two piece suit, a white blouse formed beautifully by the rise of her voluptuous breasts, accompanied by her long legs with pretty ankles springing from her black patent stiletto shoes.

The pretty young ladies blonde wavy hair dramatically pulled back from her attractive features into a bun at the back of her head, she cast a sideways glance; flashing captivating blue eyes at the older man sitting beside her. Then she turned her head to admire the view in front of her and the activities of the ducks at his feet.

The young lady spoke with an attractive low soft northern brogue in a voice loud enough to be mistaken for talking to herself, but not too loud for anybody to overhear.

"Well I received your message, what is it you want?"

The man answered without moving his head or even pausing from feeding the ducks,

"The same reason as we met your brother, we need what we paid for; you are aware of the time your brother was given to return the artefacts to us?"

"I can say nothing because I know nothing; my brother has all the answers!"

Again the elderly man spoke almost like a zombie, his face expressionless,

"I think you ought to tell your brother you will die first, I promise you, it will not be quick."

A note of real agitation crept in her voice; the coarseness of her answer blew away the sweetness of her soft brogue; shattering her lady like ambience,

"So how the fuck am I supposed to make my brother give you what you want, fuck off and see him, this has nothing to do with me; why can't you understand that! The worry is upsetting my working life!" The old man smiled then turned his head to look at the young lady as he spoke,

"Calm yourself, we do not want everybody knowing our business. Please don't let it stop you earning money; we wouldn't want the wheels of commerce grinding to a stand still."

The young lady pouted her cheeks in a sulky anger,

"Don't take the piss, all that talk about the wheels of industry. Just remember I've had your prick in my hand you old prat—perhaps I should have pulled it off."

The elderly man coughed into his curled fingers then smiled as he answered

"I might also add I thoroughly enjoyed it; you *are* very good. Nevertheless, just do as you're told; do speak to that brother of yours then you'll be safe. So go off home like a good girl, please do not annoy me any more!"

"Just try to be a little understanding you old fart! No wonder they call you bloody Donald, by the way you feed your feathered friends it should be Donald bloody duck!"

The girl stood up and walked away, her mind in absolute turmoil; although her face showed no emotion, Teresa fearfully appreciated she was being dragged into something that was endangering her life. As much as she loved her brother Moses, again and again inwardly she cursed him, for he was always able to twist her around his little finger.

The prostitute made her way back to the flat in Soho, she was one of a few who worked without a pimp, her brother had seen to that, showing his talents with guns and muscles in the area. But at this moment, when she felt so frighteningly alone; she wished she had a pimp to protect her from animals such as Mister Bloody Donald Duck! As for Donald, he'd already formulated a potful of trouble for the aggravating northern assassin; he was at this very moment making the final arrangements to implement vicious retaliations against the ex-French legionnaire.

CHAPTER 7
Tools for the Job

Pilgrim sat in the newly found rented apartment amid the Spartan style worn furnishing; running his hand over the smooth barrel of one of the weapons he'd managed to secure from an old army associate. He was like a child with a new toy, he could not believe how lucky he was; because this weapon was an elitist tool complete with silencer, the 9mm Sig-Sauer P226— Pilgrim knew it well; handling it as if it was a baby. He managed to get two of them, plus a good supply of ammunition.

His old comrade was pleased to see Pilgrim, but Pilgrim didn't like this old companion very much, he was always a bit sadistic when they were in the SAS. Pilgrim always felt that violence in some walks of life unavoidable, but not to be enjoyed, unless you wanted to end up on the funny farm; sometimes he got the impression his old associate was a just a step away from that end!

That's how Pilgrim knew this character would have what he wanted; he also managed to acquire a good pair of binoculars to be used day or night. The array of weaponry this guy showed him was awesome, the readies they had in their pockets opened another door to this man's personal armoury.

After Pilgrim had handed over the cash to this old friend Mitchell, he threw him a knife; Pilgrim caught it then tucked into his belt at his back.

"You can have that as a discount for the cash payment; you always were good with a throwing knife."

Chip glanced at Pilgrim with a shocked look on his face, prompting him to remark,

"There's a lot I don't know about you."

All these remarks run through Pilgrim's mind, triggering heavy memories from the past. Pilgrim looked over to Chip, Chip was sleeping, it was his turn to stay awake.

Pilgrim knew this weapon well and handled it like a pro, in moments he'd stripped it down, put it back together again and reloaded it. Then sat stroking it like a pet dog, Pilgrim wouldn't have admitted it but he felt safer now he was tooled up. He looked at his watch; it was three in the morning.

Hmm danger time he thought, Pilgrim was sitting at the window in a darkened room overlooking the street, now and again picking up the binoculars to scan the area; watching the wind and the rain. Several individuals were hurrying home from a late night out, Pilgrim smiled as he spotted a couple of drunks arguing, as they staggered along on their way home.

He heaved a huge sigh, the inactivity of the last few days were beginning to get to him and he knew it. The northern gangster was never out of his thoughts so—perhaps it was the old feelings from the streets, which kept creeping back into his mind; the fearful sense of terrible insecurity. Especially when he remembered the condition of one of his comrades, when the fascist organisation had finished with him; suffering many hours of torture at the hands of these so called patriots!

The need to survive that stirred old instincts as he picked up his glasses once more to scan the rain swept streets; he noticed the arrival of two taxis stopping at the kerb outside his dwelling. Three big men got out of each cab paid the driver, then hurried across the street like a herd of elephants to enter their building. Pilgrim put down the glasses to waken his partner,

"Come on I think we've got some action."

Chip sat up quickly answering,

"Why what's wrong?"

"I dunno I'm not sure, but I think its plan A."

Chip was partly dressed so he only took a minute to be fully clothed, he also pulled on a similar pair of leather gloves as Pilgrim, they then left the room to go up to the roof; turning up their collars against the rain as they walked across the flat area; Their movements were all pre-planned, so moving over to the edge of the roof, they noted once again the adjacent building, was only five feet away almost level with the one they were on. They both backed away from the edge, Pilgrim looked at Chip as he asked the poignant question!

"Do you want to go first?"

Chip smiled through the rain nodding and then Chip ran at the gap and jumped, landing easily on the other side, Pilgrim quickly followed but first taking off the night binoculars then laying them down in the box gutter that ran around the top of the roof. The roof, on which they had just landed, had a half a metre high parapet wall running the length and breadth, one metre in from the outside edge.

Pilgrim and Chip lay down behind it on the safe side, grunting as they did for the roof was rain sodden which instantly soaked into their clothes reaching their skin. They stretched out flat in a prone position facing the building they had just left; this enabled them to peep over the wall at any invaders daring to join them.

Pilgrim like Chip pulled the Sig-Sauers from their shoulder holsters; Pilgrim knew it had no orthodox safety catch, you just squeezed harder to override it; feeling even more that this was the tool to do the job—if there was a job to be done on this dirty wet cold morning.

The time hung, they felt as if they had laid in the wet and cold for an hour; but it was only ten minutes, Pilgrim looked at his watch again—grimaced but said nothing. Chip could imagine these thugs kicking open the door of their room, to find nothing and no one. While most likely then they would feel cheated, prompting these thugs to wreck what furniture existed in the frugal conditions they'd just left..

"This could be a false alarm."

Pilgrim answered again without looking away from the opposite wall.

"Chip you could be right, but on the other hand you could be dead wrong and I mean dead wrong. I'll tell you something else, if this is not a false alarm it means these people know exactly where we are. This also shows, we've been watching them watching us, there must be a traitor back at that old mansion we left up the A1."

Chip frowned at the thought of such treachery as he answered,

"There has to be an informer as you say."

Suddenly Pilgrim's muscles stiffened, he thought at first it was a trick of light bouncing around from passing vehicles head lights, but then it was accompanied by another shadow, another man circled around the other end and froze, as if waiting for an attack.

This proved instantly to Pilgrim and Chip they didn't know the whereabouts of their enemy, a slight smile slipped across Chips face as he too knew the enemy were lost; knowing he and Pilgrim had the advantage.

It started to rain heavily making visibility difficult, they could just make out the shapes of the enemy, Pilgrim fingered his new toy, tempted to chance a shot, but knew that would be a mistake. The waiting game went on for another ten minutes before one of the thugs stood up to speak in a low voice,

"This is a waste of time there's nobody around, we're getting fucking wet for no good reason!"

The individual, who spoke turned around and left the roof area via the way he came. Pilgrim and Chip heard the words quite clearly knowing this also could be a cat and mouse game, they smiled to each other but never moved a muscle!

Another ten minutes passed when suddenly through the light; one of the thugs ran and tried to jump over the gap to where they lay. Fortunately Pilgrim fired when he was in mid air, hitting him in the chest twice, causing the flying thug to lose momentum falling short of his landing area.

The unfortunate victim fell three floors to the ground below; the only good thing was he fell silently, disappearing as if by magic in the darkness; so he must have died instantly. Again the roof area fell silent while a waiting game ensued, but Pilgrim and Chip felt the enemy knew they were in an obvious disadvantaged position.

Pilgrim felt a little numb inside, pleased with himself that he'd fired and hit the thug dead centre, with the killing and dying; a package of nightmares and skeletons came zooming in from the past. Pilgrim shook his head to clear his brain, or was it his conscience?

"Good shooting mate."

He acknowledged the whispered remark from Chip with, a nod—then resumed his concentrated stare to the roof opposite. Apart from the cold and the wet, Pilgrim and Chip could hold out all night; what was left of it. Wondering what time dawn would break; Pilgrim moved closer to Chip so he could whisper unheard.

"The thugs are going to do one of two things, either they will go home or they will enter the building we're on, and then try to gain access to the roof area; in which case we need to move our positions."

Chip nodded as he answered,

"I'll go for that, what would you intend doing?"

"Well Chip one of us needs to go back to the other side of the roof, while you move to where the parapet wall makes an "L" shape on the corner of this roof. This time you lay on the drop side of the roof shielded from the area entrance, where they're most likely to burst upon us."

"Okay Pilgrim I'll do that—are you sure you want to take the risk of going back to the other roof? They might still be there."

"I know that, it's just a chance I'll have to take."

Chip shrugged his shoulders, his face showing real concern.

"Okay, if you're certain—we are fighting for our lives here, so desperate situations call for desperate acts; I'll see you later."

Chip ran to the position they'd discussed while Pilgrim stood up and moved back further from the edge of the wall to start his jump. As Pilgrim flew through the air he flinched waiting for the inevitable bullet from one of the waiting gang.

Fortunately it never came, the gamble worked, they now had both roof entrances covered. Pilgrim glanced at the luminous figures of his watch; it read three thirty, he yearned for the break of dawn, knowing the first rays of sunlight would send these thugs scurrying away like Dracula's servants.

Again it was a waiting game, the chill of wet clothes beginning to freeze to the marrow. Pilgrim and Chip yearning for the luxuries of a power shower with gallons of hot water cascading over them. Pilgrim was crouched behind a tall air conditioning vent; from where he was he could see Chip, which pleased him, that way he could give covering fire if necessary. As he scanned the roof area he noticed the slight movement from the roof access door.

Pilgrim thought to himself, surely they wouldn't think we'd stay in the same positions as before. If they did they must be very thick, but on the other the hand I must not take anything for granted. Pilgrim's mental wanderings were broken by further movement of the door, followed by the entrance of a burly figure.

Pilgrim didn't waste any time he fired immediately the man came into view, the pistol spat its venom, the injured man cried out disappearing into the darkness. The silence that followed was so quiet it was outrageously noisy almost deafening.

Pilgrim was sure there was nobody left on the other side now, bearing in mind eight thugs entered the building originally, I know I've hit two of them he thought, I'll bet the other's have run for it. So Pilgrim once again took the chance of jumping to the other side of the building then walking over to the door where the thug had fallen; he was joined by Chip. No corpse was there; obviously his partner had dragged him away. Pilgrim looked at Chip

"I think we'd better go!" Chip shrugged answering,

"I think so to, I know a very good little all night Sauna at Kings Cross, and if you're really good you can get a little hand relief from a nice little blonde."

They both burst out laughing making their way from the roof area, the two men went down the same way they came up, first entering the doorway on the roof, which brought them to the hall landing of the top floor. Then down the steps to the ground level, which was ten flights of steps. As they tripped down the stairs, both the boys were in a good mood about the success of their first confrontation; they were stopped in their tracks as they surveyed the bunch of thugs waiting for them.

The amazing point was both parties stood for several seconds just eyeing each other in absolute silence, the largest of the thugs who fronted the opposition stepped forward as he spoke, he was very tall broad shouldered also he was holding a long bladed knife; bearing in mind he was a step lower than our two heroes but he was still taller!

"Did you really think you would be able to disappear after killing a couple of our mates, we are going to smash you two to pulp, no guns 'cos of the law; we will finish you two with our bare hands!" As he finished speaking he waved the knife around in a menacing manner. Pilgrim's eyes noted almost automatically the grievous ugliness that always spreads across the faces of these examples of dissolute characters, that were about to try to kill them!

Pilgrim knew he had to get really close very quickly to contain the big guy with the knife, stepping forward then striking quickly his wrist with the edges of both of the palms of his hands in a chopping action, which managed to dislodge his grasp sending the knife cluttering down the stairs. He then threw himself forward to head butt the giant broken nosed spokesman good and hard; sending him spinning back into his followers spitting blood and snot over his fellow aggressors.

After that they paused for a second, and then the rest of the eight strong gang who opposed them suddenly charged as one unit up the stairs in a determined effort to totally and physically destroy their enemy. Not having time to draw their guns, Chip and Pilgrim started to fight for their lives, their pumping fists spreading more blood and snot.

An interesting tactical error on their part was that Pilgrim and Chip had the advantage of the high ground, added to that the width of the stair enabled only three people at a time to pass through their ranks to attack them; the rest hindered the progressive action of their own assailants!

Pilgrim and Chip were very large specimens of proven ability at the roughhouse fisticuffs, due to the vicious struggle to survive as ex coppers; in the harsh stamping grounds of her Majesties Prisons. The two ex lawmen's arms pumped out devastating punches like heavyweight boxers; their feet and heads along with their knees working in fruitful destructive coalition.

Raining bloody punishment down on these would be warriors of the night, which was gradually breaking the enemy's spirit. One of the larger guys was giving Pilgrim a hard time; it was only the continued weight of the non stop punching by Pilgrim that gradually caused this giant to slip to the rear of the melee.

Pilgrim knew they were winning when one of them tried to pull a gun in desperation, which was knocked out of his hand, landing on the step by the side of him, which he just about managed to kick away.

The spinning revolver sailed down the stairs through the legs of the attackers, spitting out bullets as it tumbled spinning amongst the combat of grunting sweating bodies with groaning swearing mouths; several of the thugs stumbled to the floor as they received the sporadic spitting bullets from the flying weapon!

Suddenly from below they could all hear the noise of Police sirens, hoping it was not for them; but of course it was! Where upon the thugs broke away from the skirmish dragging their wounded with them as they ran off down the stairs in full retreat, they of course realising the accidental firing of the gun had brought the unwanted boys in blue to the stairway of blood and thunder.

No doubt the gunfire earlier was ignored but obviously this latter shot was one blast too many, the local inhabitants were obviously worried and frightened by the noise of the fighting directly outside their doors.

The thugs all started to gallop down the stairs in the vain optimism of evading capture; Pilgrim and Chip run up the stairs to the flat roof area. There they peeped over the edge to see the whereabouts of the Police; about ten to twelve armed officers were running in to the building.

So Pilgrim and Chip looked at each other then quickly walked to look over to the other roof, first both men walked to the back side of the building to drop their weapons over the edge into a small yard space; then they both broke into a sprint to jump once more onto the adjacent flat roofed area. They quickly walked over to the edge of that roof then estimated the jump to the next roof, but it was certainly too far.

"Pilgrim whether we like it or not we have to stay in this building and take a chance."

Pilgrim shrugged his shoulders as he answered,

"Yeah I suppose so, but let's just stay up here until we are forced to go down; they might just leave us here! We could do with a bit of luck; you never know we might get away with it."

Pilgrim and Chip laid down on the roof edge to watch the thugs who attacked them being escorted out of the building into a Black Maria. In fact they were so interested in watching the activities of the Police on the ground floor, they were more than surprised to hear a voice ordering them to lay flat and spreadeagle.

Pilgrim cast a sideways glance at Chip as he murmured,

"I don't fucking believe this."

The two men were also accompanied to the ground then also escorted into a waiting Police car, in no time at all Pilgrim with Chip were sitting in separate cells for charges to be levelled against them. What worried Pilgrim, he was already out on parole so it looked very likely he was heading back to jail to finish his sentence for breaking his parole orders.

The only good thing about all this was he and Chip certainly knew the drill for avoiding Police questioning, after all they had been trained in the rigid procedure. So all Pilgrim could do was like Chip sit and wait, in fact he lay down on the bed then actually started to drop off to sleep!

Approximately two hours later the cell door opened then an individual walked in to stand and stare at Pilgrim for several moments before he spoke, he was a slim smart young pragmatic looking individual, brown eyes with black hair neatly parted brushed flat.

"I don't suppose you remember me Pilgrim; I was one of your underlings at one time before you transferred to M I 6."

Pilgrim sat up from the prone position to study the man at the door. Pilgrim smiled nodding as he answered quietly.

"Oh yes I remember you, the bright university lad, your name is Roberts; how could I forget you?"

It was the turn of the man at the door to smile and he did.

"I could and never will believe you were guilty of killing your colleague Pilgrim, you and I know how certain forensic can be fixed up to suit the occasion! I haven't got a clue what you were doing in that building earlier, but one thing is for sure, if there are questions to be asked you will go straight back to the nick; I certainly owe you more than that. So you had better get your arse out of here before people of a higher rank than me appear at the station to keep you here. You had better take the other guy with you."

The young man at the door stood to one side, smiled then winked at one of his heroes as he came nearer, who when he was a young newcomer to CID, had his life saved by the man he was now setting free. Pilgrim stopped suddenly to shake the hand of this once young lad who was now a man who held him in high esteem.

The sequence of events flashed back into Pilgrim's mind as if it was yesterday, Pilgrim was called to investigate reports of a probable terrorist firearms cache in a barge on the Thames. The young inexperienced entrant was ordered to accompany him to the floating arsenal, only because it was within their Policing zone.

When he with the young man ventured aboard, Pilgrim went below—the boy stayed on the deck, what Pilgrim saw was a booby trap for any unwanted visitors. More than likely set off by them the moment they boarded the smelly hulk. Pilgrim moved back topside as fast as he could, running at the boy jumping into the water taking the lad with him.

When both of them were floating in the water next to the barge, Pilgrim shouted at the lad to dive with him as deep as he could. The following explosion was enormous, only the quick thinking action by Pilgrim saved their lives, something the young man could never forget! As Pilgrim left the cell he stopped to ask the younger man a favour.

"Would you please phone to speak to a man called Peter Miles at M I 6, ask him to expect a phone call from me, I would really appreciate that small favour."

The young inspector smiled nodding as he answered,

"Of course I will."

Pilgrim along with Chip was quick to shake the dust of the Police station from their shoes, quickly making their way back to where the car was parked. Conscious of the bruises they were carrying which were painful when they walked; happily the small amount of damage they received was only superficial; luckily on the lower part of their torsos; fortunately their wedding tackle was in good order!

Both men discussed the obvious situation that they were followed from the mansion, proving there was positively a sneak informer in the ranks there. Pilgrim commented to Chip how lucky he was to still be free, explaining the fortuitous meeting with the lad who owed him his life; but said nothing of the problems that put him in prison! It was very reassuring to climb into their car once more, causing their spirits to be lifted as they drove off to the all night sauna.

Dawn was breaking throwing her well rehearsed act across London, as they walked down the Marylebone Road, after parking the car in a deserted side street. It had stopped raining; it was surprising how many people were around at that time of the morning; then they crossed the road to the all night sauna.

"Pilgrim I don't know which is worse the hunger, the wet clothes or the lack of sleep!"

Pilgrim laughed as he answered,

"Well you have a good choice."

The entrance to the Sauna was by a long corridor, poorly lit, and painted the same way, opening out to a receptionist's desk. Behind the desk sat a pretty girl of Thai origins, she greeted them with a big smile,

"What do you want gentlemen? You'll find we have a lot to offer—boys or girls plus sauna and massage."

The two sauna candidates smiled, Chip answering first with the words.

"Just a sauna with a massage thanks."

"Do you both want the same?"

Pilgrim let Chip do the talking while he just stood there admiring the beautiful young lady.

"Oh yes, but separately, first my colleague then me, while he's in there I'll wait until it's my turn—okay."

The beauty behind the counter looked at the men with a puzzled look on her face then answered,

"Anything you say—you're paying."

She rang a bell on the counter, then they were quickly being accompanied to their destination, which was a curtained compartment containing a massage table for Pilgrim; for Chip the similar set up opposite while he waited.

Chip moved back to sit on the massage table in his own curtained area, for he like Pilgrim was beginning to feel very weary. Chip cast his thoughts back to the flat they'd just vacated in a hurry, mentally checking systematically what they'd left there, but was satisfied that nothing of any importance could be found by their enemies.

The mental condition of running his mind over the past was a left over from the police force, a habit he was quite happy to maintain. Chip thought about the Spartan style dressing of the room, the way the furniture in rented hotel rooms always seemed to tell the same story.

He smiled at his own thoughts, it was as if even the furniture knew it was hired and not bought from a burst of loving power to establish a home or a cherished love nest. When his life was filled with a passion engulfing him like a raging fire with the prostitute who led to his fall from grace, it was always in his mind the uncharitable aura of rented rooms intruding into the magic that surrounded them at the time.

Chips thoughts were now interrupted by the sound of a cultured voice addressing Pilgrim that possessed a note of menace. Chip's hand moved to pull from his holster the weapon that had served them so well, waiting to hear more, unfortunately it was not there! So moving closer to the curtain then carefully pulling back the drapes to peer through to Pilgrim, but he still could not see anything.

So Chip glanced up and down the corridor outside of the compartments, then stepped into the corridor dividing them, again moving closer to gently move the curtain apart.

Chip could see Pilgrim laying on his back naked as the day he was born, which brought a smile to Chip's face, by the side of him stood the Japanese girl, looking very frightened. All eyes were on this elderly man speaking with the cultured voice in a threatening tone.

Chip decided to listen for a while; as he was listening his eyes roved hungrily searching for something that could imitate the convincing feel of a revolver. Suddenly he saw on a nearby desk an asthma inhaler, he quickly tiptoed over to it scooped it up; returning to stand once again listening to the threatening tones of the man in the suit. The man with the cultured voice cleared his throat.

"I'm sorry to disturb you at this time but unfortunately you are beginning to be a pest and you will have to be removed. We know who employs you; we will of course in time remove this man as well."

The cultured killer moved his hand, it was obvious he was going to take a gun from his pocket; Chip could not take any more chances, so he pushed his asthma inhaler through the curtain into the back of the man's head, addressing the aggressor in a quiet menacing voice.

"Please stand very still, and then slowly put your hands on top of your head, if you do not do this I will blow you're fucking head right off!"

The man did as he was told immediately, Chip told the Japanese girl also to stand very still. Chip did not see the point of some hysterical girl running off to call the police, or worse still her minders.

"Pilgrim you'd better go and put your clothes on, I'll wait here with the girl then we'll decide what to do with this vermin when you get back."

It wasn't long before Pilgrim was back, they both stood looking at this elderly man dressed like an office worker; but had the aura of an assassin.

"Pilgrim I think we ought to take him with us."

Pilgrim nodded his head as he spoke.

"Yes so do I, in fact this could be our lucky day, he might be elderly but I'll till squeeze his bollocks to get the truth out of him; I'll take his weapon from him first!"

Pilgrim smiling recognising the deadly asthma inhaler, as he quickly went over the hostage's body to find in his inside pocket a snub nosed Smith and Weston; Pilgrim took the weapon pushing it into the hands of Chip.

"Come on let's go Chip."

Pilgrim and Chip left the sauna, taking the educated thug with them, not before telling the management they did not want any Police involved, or they would be back with a few hand grenades! These empty threats from them changed the facial complexion of the eastern character that owned the brothel. They made the killer walk in front of them, assuring the prisoner if he attempted to escape; he would definitely get a bullet in his back.

A short journey in the car brought them outside another flat unknown to their enemies, this time it was a block in Knightsbridge; a better quality property completely. The two bed roomed flat was on the fourth floor, the carpeted hallways of the building had a lift; which at this moment was waiting for them. It was still fairly early so there was very few people up or around in the building generally.

They let themselves in then sat the old boy down in a chair prior to discussing what was to be done with him. Pilgrim knew exactly what to do with him, he proceeded to take a rope from under the sink, placed there by them earlier, taking it to then tie the end of the rope to the handle of the bedroom door; throwing the loose end over the opposite side. When Pilgrim was ready he called Chip,

"Bring that old bastard over here, but try to push him close up against the door; while I tie this noose around his neck." Chip looked a little shocked at Pilgrim.

"Steady on Pilgrim I don't want to kill him yet."

The old boy sneered at Chip.

"I knew you wouldn't have the courage to kill me."

Pilgrim stepped forward and threw the noose over the man's head saying as he did,

"He might not have, but I have you old bastard!"

At that Pilgrim pulled hard on the rope then tied it off back over around the handle of the door again on the opposite side. This pulled the killer up onto his toes, unfortunately for him he had to stay there or choke, the old boy squirmed.

"You cannot leave me like this I'll die!"

"Then die you bastard or tell us what we want, we'll drink our tea first, just to give you time to think it all out. We want the answer to two questions the first one is; wait for it! Who is the informer at the manor in Grantham? Secondly where is the assassin, who is known as Moses Dolan?

Think long and hard, because I've more exciting ways to make you just that bit more uncomfortable. Oh and this one is the easiest, that is for you I mean; added to this I think I'll tie your hands behind your back."

Pilgrim spun the suspended man around to face the door, bumping and knocking his face as he did so; then quickly tied his hands together behind his back; that tightened the rope suspending him even higher. Chip stood watching Pilgrim during what one might call his appraisal of the situation, then walked away to the kitchen to make the tea murmuring to himself;

"God knows we've earned one."

Pilgrim followed him; Chip looked and sounded a bit worried,

"I don't want to kill him Pilgrim."

"I tell you what, that bastard was going to slot me with out a thought, so don't spare any pity for that old man, if necessary I'll throw him out of the window when we're finished with him."

Chip was staring at Pilgrim with a look of surprise and horror on his face, "What's a matter with you Pilgrim, are you going crazy?"

"No I'm not going crazy, I just don't know how to handle this situation any other way, the old boy who gave us this job was right, these guys are filth. They are the dregs of the world; I intend treating them for what they are! Do you object?"

Chip never answered right away, but thought for a moment letting a few seconds slide by.

"Well I understand what you're saying but just don't go too strong."

"Look old friend I sense you're getting jittery over a little violence, I've seen it before in a comrade you might say. Please just relax; but just remember that bastard was going to kill me in cold blood, only a wild animal would do that. I've come across this before, I know the only way to handle these characters is to give them what they deserve; otherwise they think you're a fool."

Chip rolled his eyes in acceptance of the situation,

"Okay, Okay—I know you're right, it's just that I'm used to keeping it all within the law."

Chip proceeded to make the tea then they both sat down, they were both now very tired.

"Pilgrim I think you need some sleep, so get your head down while I watch the old man."

Pilgrim stared at Chip with a severe look on his face as he spoke,

"If you are soft with that old bastard he'll kill us both, I hope you remember that. I also think the difference between us is, I ended up in the SAS handling violence differently to you.

After all you were a policeman who had to abide by the law; I think that must become a habit. I know we were meant to stay in a certain strait jacket of democracy, but—now and then we'd go beyond it but not very often and not very much; that's why we lost the fight some times. Well now we can go as far over the top as we have to, please don't go soft on me now."

Chip smiled,

"I'm sorry—I know you're right, don't worry if he so much as farts I'll kill him."

Pilgrim thought for a moment,

"Would you prefer to interrogate him now?"

Chip looked round quickly at Pilgrim answering almost immediately,

"Yes, I would like that, let's do it now. I know you're tired but it has to be done."

"I agree Chip, when it's done we can throw him out of the window." Pilgrim winked then smiled, knowing the old man could hear them, he thought it would frighten him. They stood in front of the candidate, just staring at him for a while before saying a word. The old man was beginning to look a little worse for wear, being kept on his tiptoes certainly did not agree with him; not that it would agree with anyone! Pilgrim spoke with venom in his voice,

"Right! Where is Moses Dolan living?"

The old man's eyes flashed full of hatred for the men who stood before him, but the position he was in, he knew it would not help himself to anger them further!

"I really don't know where he actually lives, but I can tell you where he's staying at the moment."

"Well you can just do that my friend; I just hope you're telling the truth for your sake. Who is the informer at the mansion?"

The old man rolled his eyes moaning before answering,

"I really don't know, if I did I'd tell you."

Pilgrim smiled at Chip,

"I thought he was going to help us, well I'll just have to tighten the rope a bit more. Hang on to him Chip while I hoist him up a bit more." Pilgrim walked to the back of the door and started to pull on the rope, the old man remained silent. Chip moved to the back of the door where Pilgrim was putting his hand on Pilgrim shaking his head speaking softly.

"That's enough mate he's too scared to talk anymore."

Pilgrim shrugged his shoulders also speaking in a low voice,

"Okay, perhaps you're right, I'll tell you what; let's get him to take us to where the Paddy lives, then perhaps we can dump him off somewhere."

Chip nodded, agreeing also looking relieved,

"Okay we'll do it."

Pilgrim didn't know how much longer he could keep going he was nearing to total exhaustion. Before they could leave the flat they carefully cleaned away all of the fingerprints; then took great care to remove all personal belongings, then securely loaded the old man into the car.

They tied him up securely in the front passenger's seat, while Chip sat behind with his revolver; ready to scatter his brains if necessary. The old man directed them to a flat in the East End of London in Whitechapel, the two of them were undecided what to do, so they got out of the car to discuss the problem; the problem being the front seat passenger.

"Chip I think we can just drive up the M11 for a while about twenty five miles to Bishops Stortford or somewhere, empty his pockets, take off his shoes leave him barefoot; in an isolated place. We can't kill him, I know in my heart we should; and I'm certain in the very near future we are going to be sorry for not finishing him off. I suppose we'll deal with that when it occurs."

Chip looked at Pilgrim and again he nodded feeling like a nodding dog,

"Pilgrim old friend I'm too tired to argue with anybody; at this moment I can't think of anything better than that."

Pilgrim thought to himself as he was driving, if they were not so tired we could have left the old gangster tied up, while they slept. But and it was very big but, if this guy managed to get out of his ropes while they slept soundly, there was no way they were ever going to wake up again.

At last the two boys found the spot to dump the old fool, warning him if they ever saw him again they would kill him instantly. The threat was only met with sneers from this dangerous assassin, who threw mocking insults and threats at them as they drove away; the old gangster could not resist one more stabbing taunt at Pilgrim.

His mind full of hatred and disappointment that two young men of their calibre could catch such an experienced criminal as him, he wanted to hurt them and at the same time deep down demand recognition as a senior within his own twisted world. The old boy knew exactly what would definitely catch Pilgrim's attention, so he blurted out the one remark he knew would make the younger man listen!

"At least I know who fitted you up with murder, you young know all wanker!"

On hearing these mordant jibes, Pilgrim's foot stabbed the brake pedal as quick as lightning, then he leapt out of the car to chase this vulpine character down the road; catching him easily as the skinny pensioner tried to sprint barefooted but ended up hopping and swearing trying to rub his sensitive battered feet!

Pilgrim's curiosity was now burning bright, but as angry and as curious as he was, he could not help laughing at the hilarious figure in front of him; hopping about as if he was on a red hot stove. Pilgrim caught the old reprobate by the throat as he demanded all that the man knew about this particular carbuncle in Pilgrim's life. Even though he was almost choking, he still could not resist the last sneering remarks before submission.

"That really did attract your attention didn't it, you clever bollocks!" Pilgrim's hand around the man's throat tightened, he was quick to demand a little mercy in a squealing voice,

"If you strangle me you will never know who it was that fixed up the forensic evidence."

"Who was it you sneering rat?"

"Alright—alright!"

Squeaked the old man,

"I'll tell you, only the next time you see me, remember you owe me you young wanker. His nickname is Slippery Sam, from Bow in the East End of London."

Pilgrim dragged him back to the car now stopped in the middle of the road, still with its head lights on. Pilgrim then called to Nick sitting there watching the comedy in the head lights of the car, unaware of the poignancy of the remarks from the freed prisoner, nevertheless he still frisked around in the car to find a pencil and paper, to then hurriedly passed them to Pilgrim.

"Now you old bastard what is the address of this character? Make it the truth otherwise I'll forget I'm working for the man in Grantham and spend my time finding and killing you, make sure everything you write is correct otherwise you will die when I catch you!"

With these last words spoken, Pilgrim aggressively thrust his face into the flaccid features of the now terrified barefoot killer; who now wished he had said nothing. So grabbing the pencil and paper from the threatening figure in front of him, he proceeded to scribble the address along with a short description of the wanted miscreant. When he was finished, Pilgrim snatched the slip of paper from him, jumped into the car then accelerated away from the barefoot scoundrel amidst a volley of foul mouthed abuse!

Pilgrim was now finding it hard to stop from falling asleep as he was driving, his body was in open revolt, it demanded sleep; poor Chip was in no better state. After a good few miles were distanced between them and the unwanted companion, they found a hotel. The hotel was down a long dark lane, still in leafy suburbia, the boys booked into two different rooms at different ends of the corridor.

Then settled down to sleep in the same room after jamming a chair under the handle of the door; then finding miscellaneous articles to scatter about the floor, by the time they went to sleep the floor was like a mine field. Pilgrim and Chip slipped from this world to sleep soundly for eight solid hours.

CHAPTER 8
What Is Going on in There?

They awoke in a panic, worried that much might have happened while they were sleeping. The drive back to London didn't promise any problems, the boys themselves never had a lot to say; the difficulty of capturing a clever professional like Moses the hit man made them wonder, if it was perhaps becoming too much for them!

Pilgrim mentally shrugged it off thinking to himself no doubt the opportunity of detaining this man would emerge, it always does he thought. As for the address that the old man had given him only given because of his imprisonment, he really wondered, if this was going to be the break he had dreamed of getting; I have to hope it is genuine.

As for Chip he was off somewhere else, thinking of the last occurrences during the confrontation with the villains. Pilgrim's thoughts wandered off to the man called "Slippery Sam," but he momentarily thought of the gangster who fell off the roof with a bullet in him!

"Chip, I wonder what the law thought of the body that fell from the roof when they found it?"

"I wouldn't worry about that too much, what with drugs and protection coupled with the general crime in London; an odd body now and again won't raise any eyebrows."

Pilgrim shook his head as he answered,

"I suppose not."

"There is one thing that is worrying and that is the old boy's gun, we could end up in prison for a murder he committed."

Pilgrim murmured a few words of agreement. So he took the weapon from his pocket, putting it into a plastic bag he took from the glove compartment, after painstakingly taking it apart then very carefully wiping it clean. At that time they were passing open land, so Chip stopped to let Pilgrim wander into the field to toss the weapon into the bushes, the two of them felt a lot safer now the problem of the gun was dealt with; they then drove on in the general direction of London.

"The question is Chip, what are we going to do next? We slept for eight hours, giving that old bastard the time to contact anybody in the world. So now Moses the assassin might well be alerted to our intended course of action, we will need to change our procedure; so I'm sure it would be wiser to concentrate on the Paddy's sister."

"I agree Pilgrim, we must go for taking the prostitute hostage, haul her around with us, or we could just watch her flat. For I'm sure, that's where the Paddy will more than likely show up. By the way, what was that address the old man gave you? You know to whom I'm referring, the old git we dropped off up the motor way; the old fool that was hopping about like a cat on a hot tin roof."

They both laughed together as they recalled the sight of the unrehearsed comedy act, as for Pilgrim he answered with a big grin on his face,

"How could I ever forget that little dancing act?"

Pilgrim then explained in detail, telling Chip that the name he squeezed out of the old git was Slippery Sam, who according to the old man was directly responsible for the production of fraudulent evidence; that seemingly if the old man was truthful, lives at Bow in the East End of London. Pilgrim looked a little puzzled as he asked,

"What actually are you referring to, when you say evidence, what manufactured evidence?"

"I'm sorry Chip it's something I have never spoken about. All this is to do with the falsified forensic evidence that initially condemned me to prison; for the death of my colleague John Tregear. To stumble on such an important piece of information like this is certainly heaven sent, I know I certainly did not kill Trigger; the presentation to the court with this damning forensic evidence left me stunned. I never ever thought I would solve this mysterious data that destroyed me."

Chip was very surprised and interested, so then he asked,

"Why didn't you tell me when we were in prison, about all this web of lies and deceit that surrounded you?"

Pilgrim smiled rolling his eyes as he answered,

"What was the point of it, everybody you spoke to in there was innocent and only in prison because they were fitted up by the Police! So within that environment who would be interested in just another whinger?"

Chip nodded as he spoke,

"I understand."

Pilgrim then explained the rest of the story,

"I fortunately hid away a large amount of collated evidence compiled by me and Trigger against the politicians who were entangled with all this villainy; but decided against presenting it at the time because of the enemy who cleverly discredited my status as an agent. Who knows perhaps the time is coming, when I will have the opportunity of revealing this jaw dropping material!"

Chip stroked his chin heaving a huge sigh as he spoke,

"Let's hope so, I am really surprised by this revelation of yours, I thought I was the only one with problems from the past; I always thought yours was all cut and dried."

A solemn quietness fell between the two friends, as they followed the road to London; for as much as they were confused as to actually who they should follow tripping across their minds, they as individuals were still haunted by demons from their own past. Pilgrim after many miles were eaten up, was the first to break the shroud of silence,

"I've suddenly realised we have a problem, we are short of weapons; I think we should give my friend Mitch a call."

"Okay I'll go for that, it would be a good idea to do that before we do anything else."

"Absolutely Chip, but I've changed my mind as to what weapon I want, now that I know how the enemy performs. I think they will come at us in greater numbers; especially now that we've definitely stirred up a Hornet's nest. When we were there the last time, I saw a nice little Uzi mini sub machine gun, it's easy to load, steady to use and I think we need that sort of fire power."

Chip grinned at the details Pilgrim gave about the proposed weapon, thinking this guy was perhaps more than these enemies of ours would be able to handle.

"I'm with you Pilgrim, I think you're right."

Unnoticed by Pilgrim, Chip's smile never left his face, for it was the sincerity of Pilgrim's words that amused Chip! The ride to town was uneventful; they visited Pilgrim's ex comrade then came out carrying a small holdall that was full of their goodies, of Pilgrim's choice!

Lunch was the next item on the agenda, then a visit to the area where the prostitute lived. The two of them managed to secure a small flat at a very good rate opposite her premises, which was outrageously fortunate; but this time it was going to be a night and day job of surveillance.

They both felt they had been a bit unlucky on the timing of finding out where the Paddy lived; if they hadn't been in such a state of fatigue at the time, they might have grabbed him. At that time, due to their exhausted state they let it ride then hoped for another opportunity, for now of course they would have to be happy with this address; just be satisfied with either grabbing his sister; or just plain around the clock surveillance.

"Chip, I don't think we ought to enter our new flat until nightfall, we have less chance of being noticed."

"Okay Pilgrim, I know you are right; but when we are driving around I just hope we are never stopped by the boys in blue, then be put in the position of explaining to the Police why we have a tool like that."

Chip said this as he nodded to the Uzi sub-machine gun lying on the floor of the car at Pilgrim's feet! Pilgrim never answered just chuckled to himself. Nevertheless they made a point of eating across the other side of the river, on the south side of the Thames.

"Chip, do you think we might pay this character a visit that lives in the East End of London? Bearing in mind we have some time to kill prior to entering our fresh accommodation."

"Okay I have nothing against us doing that, as you say it would help to kill a bit of time anyway."

Chip and Pilgrim finished their meal then made their way to Bow in the East End of London, the journey didn't take long; and in no time at all they were standing outside Slippery Sam's flat in a multi floored council concrete tower block on the fourth floor; pressing the door bell.

A small sartorially dressed man with a small moustache answered the door, his hair brushed flat across the top of his head; speaking with a slight cockney accent, but sounding his vowels in a perfect manner.

He stood there with one hand in his pocket, brushing away food from his moustached upper lip with his forefinger as he spoke;

"Yes, what do you want?"

He asked in quiet voice, Pilgrim found it hard to believe that such an ordinary civilised looking character could ever be responsible for imprisoning him for two years, with the original threat of many years longer,

"Could you tell me if a man with a reputation or name called Slippery Sam lives here? We have a message for him."

The little man hesitated for a moment before he answered, carefully eyeing up these two men standing before him,

"Yes, I could—that happens to be what they call me, such as it is; tell me the message then let me finish eating my dinner."

Pilgrim nodded as he answered, an action that was becoming a habit,

"Well seemingly the man who spoke to us was sure you would recognise this name, Garth Pilgrim, you see he was sure you had something to tell him."

Slippery Sam stood for a minute with a puzzled look on his face, then suddenly the words came together in his mind; after all it was several years ago when he wove the forensic evidence around the man who was asking him the question. But now—right now, here he was standing in front of him!

Slippery Sam realising he could very well be in deep trouble, so then he suddenly tried to slam the door in the face of the two men who really did look very large and extremely menacing; in the hope he could retreat to the inner sanctuary of his flat! Pilgrim the big lump had no trouble stopping this aggressive action happening with one foot while his large hands reached out and grabbed the little fellow by his shirt collar; lifting him out of the doorway to place him in the corridor up against the wall to join them.

"You have some serious explaining to do, bearing in mind we are four floors up, and you don't bounce!"

"It, it—was nothing personal, I don't even know you, this guy who gave me all the relevant information; he paid me good money, so then I acted on it."

"So you are ready to tell the truth to the police if I take you there? It will save your stinking life, you fucking worm do you think you could tell me the man's name?"

The suave little man seemed to shrink to even a smaller size, his speech also becoming quieter encumbered with insecurity unsure how to answer these very pertinent probing questions,

"How can I? He was working for the government and no doubt still is; an M I 6 agent. If I didn't do as he told me, then I was a goner; a dead man!"

These answers stunned Pilgrim, so all this according to this little fart was down to one of the department. One of our very own, what do I do now? Pilgrim's brain was working overtime; he badly needed to interrogate this wanker for several hours to get the real truth.

"If what you say is true, have you any evidence that this agent was part of this conspiracy? If for one moment I think you're lying then I will kill you, for I've had several years of my life stolen; to say I am bitter—is an understatement."

Sid squirmed trying to free himself from Pilgrim's grip as he answered,

"If you let go of me please, I am not a violent man, but a man of science. I work very methodically; I might have some answers for you."

The little man straightened his clothes, stretching his neck in an indignant manner. Showing his irritation of being mishandled when Pilgrim let go of him, he then turned to motion with his head; inviting his two antagonists to follow him. In such a way, it illustrated he was without doubt a complete eccentric!

When they entered, the opulence of the council flat was astounding, it was also spotlessly clean. They followed him down the hallway, stopping at what obviously was formerly a bedroom door, he unlocked it then opened the door revealing a fully fitted laboratory; in one corner were numerous filing cabinets; which looked strangely antique, which told them how long this man had been operational!

"You see I am, due to my talent forced to mix with very dangerous criminals, the only way I can protect myself from these types are by collating information on them, then placing the sealed parcelled copies with solicitors; in the event of my death they will be automatically sent to the appropriate authority."

Our two ex—policemen were duly impressed; Pilgrim could not help saying the obvious.

"It's a pity that you left your conscience with the solicitor as well!"

Sid narrowed his eyes as he answered,

"I cannot afford to have anything as expensive as a conscience."

He pulled open one of the filing cabinets draws, then took from it a folder thumbing through it,

"If I was not so fastidious I would not be able to help you."

Also they were surprised at the old fashioned method of filing. Pilgrim was absolutely stunned at the way the man was so willing to part with any information so easily.

"How can you survive if you have all this information but part with it so easily?"

Slippery Sam gave Pilgrim a look of disgust as he answered,

"How will they know? They will have no proof—then if they do kill me, no matter how clever they are; they will be indicted with all their history stored in these cabinets, which is also in other places unknown to them! Now you have been here endangering my living, I shall be gone within a few days; but have no fear I will leave here all evidence required to prove your innocence. It is my way of repaying them for their incompetence, allowing my cover to be ripped open for all to see."

The expert on the manipulation of forensics Slippery Sam; spoke the next few sentences with strong emphasis on his words,

"You must remember to do what I did to you could only be committed with the help from your department; or at least several agents within it. I can give you the names I dealt with, and then of course it's up to you. I have no need to warn you, that you are walking a very dangerous path, so if I was you, I would settle for my parole and forget all about it and live. Because I'm sure they will kill you if you become a nuisance!"

Chip looked at Pilgrim in astonishment; Pilgrim felt the same way and stood silent for several fleeting moments before reacting to these somewhat conclusive remarks.

"I don't think I can do that."

Sid stared at Pilgrim, then shrugged his shoulders as he spoke,

"That of course—is your decision; now please let me finish my dinner."

Pilgrim left the flat, with the devastating information he wanted tucked under his arm, followed by Chip without saying a word to the serpent of a man he spoke to masquerading as a human being. He was at least carrying with him two names of individuals, which did without doubt conspire to severely damage him and his family; not to mention the killing of John Tregear.

One important factor he was very sure of, he was now like a dog with a bone, certain that no matter what happened he was never going to let go; whoever and what ever threatened him. When they were sitting in their car, Chip gave Pilgrim a nudge as he was about to drive away,

"That conversation was mind boggling; to be framed by your own people is beyond belief."

Pilgrim answered without moving his head but looked straight ahead,

"You see Chip I'm convinced the bombshell of shame that engulfed my family did I'm sure cause the cancer in my wife's body; that eventually led too her death. All the trouble they went to in prefabricating evidence; must only have been to protect somebody in a very high position. We were certainly aware that a junior minister was on the payroll of drugs gangs plus a senior cabinet member, to achieve the laundering of such enormous amounts of money from government contracts; but who else was involved? Maybe we were on the edge of uncovering the biggest scandal this country has ever seen, to them the only way of stopping us was to implicate me with my colleague Tregear in some way; and as you know—they did!"

Chip really did feel sorry for Pilgrim especially the facts concerning his wife,

"So what do you intend doing now?"

"At the moment Chip, nothing—I need time to reflect, to plan and stay alive; bearing in mind the villains that surround us now. Come on we had better get to the flat to do the job we are getting paid for. Just as Pilgrim was about to drive away, he stopped, then turned his head to speak to Chip,

"Three people's lives were ruined, my very good friend Trigger was murdered, my wife died of cancer plus as you know my life ultimately torn apart; not to mention my children's well being—somebody somewhere has got to pay the price for all this misery!"

The rest of the journey was travelled in silence with both men having plenty to dwell on. Once darkness fell they entered the flat, there they agreed for Chip to do the first shift, then to awaken Pilgrim at three in the morning. Chip sat at the window in the darkened room, the night binoculars by his side with a note pad. Chip intended to write down how many clients entered the property over twenty four hours.

The last couple of hours she had received three customers now that was good business; thought Chip. He scrutinised every client, hoping to see someone who might resemble the Northern assassin hit man, the photograph lay on the small coffee table beside him for quick reference if needed; the waiting went on for more than a week.

The two observers were then undecided whether to grab the girl; then wait for her brother to arrive. Or wait for the customer they really wanted, so they sort of split the difference and did a bit of waiting and watching and hoping. Pilgrim sat alone at the window overlooking the prostitute's premises while Chip slept, Pilgrim's thoughts ran over Slippery Sam's advice, to forget all about his imprisonment for his own safety; it almost made Pilgrim choke with rage.

Who do these dissolute bastards think they are? It was outrageous to even suggest that he would be too frightened to question their derisive actions, which caused the ruination of his life. Where would I actually start? That is the burning question! Pilgrim had names, names that he knew, in fact when Pilgrim read of these fellow operatives; in his mind he felt they were incapable of such an awful deed.

Obviously this honest agent had too much respect for his fellow operators! When Pilgrim quickly scanned through the documents from Sid, he was surprised by the comprehensive information they contained; after reading it he kept asking himself where does one begin to incriminate these pair of gangsters masquerading as protectors of the state.

If Pilgrim was still employed by M I 6, it would be easy to delve into their accounts without them knowing; to check whether or not they received any payments during the time of my incarceration. Pilgrim picked up the night binoculars to once again scan the area, a week had passed still there was no sign of the assassin; what else could they do but sit and wait.

Pilgrim's mind dropped back to his own problem, on the night he was supposed to have killed his very good friend John Tregear; he spent most of the evening delving through government archives prior to his visit to see Trigger, somebody knew he was entirely alone that evening to be able to fit him up so successfully.

This man Alfred Etherington is quite a popular character amongst the media mammals, as Pilgrim liked to call the press! He is also an influential member of the cabinet, serving as the minister of health. Pilgrim really did think at the time he was on the brink of capturing this person red handed.

Then suddenly it all went wrong, but why? Why? Why? What was said to set this sequence of events in motion? Pilgrim sat for an hour racking his memory going over past events as he had done for so many years, focussing his mind on all conversations between him and Tregear prior to his death and his own arrest.

Pilgrim remembered two phone calls he made to his colleague, both those calls contained damning evidence for Paul Wenham the junior minister, the second call was the one which we agreed to, who would do what. Tregear agreed to go and search the cabinet minister's constituent's office, while I searched government archives; arranging to meet Trigger later.

The salient point was Pilgrim and Trigger only allowed themselves to speak so openly, because they were using the phones within the M I 6 headquarters. All the agents were always assured they were safe secure phone lines; after all what would be the point if the organisation's building was insecure.

Of course all the pieces of the jigsaw are gradually fitting together; the appliances must have been bugged for them to be aware of all our movements! One factor is being made very clear; they (Tregear and Pilgrim) must have been a lot closer than ever imagined and into something far bigger than they knew.

Pilgrim glanced at his watch realising it was Chip's turn at the window; he moved to the side of Chip to wake him. Pilgrim was very pleased to lie down then go to sleep, thus escaping temporarily from the problems of the waking world.

There was still one very big question that would not leave Pilgrim's brain, how the hell did the man called Tobias know he was innocent of murdering his good friend and colleague John Tregear!

The waiting and watching and hoping went on for a further ten days, until bingo the man with the right face, appeared from nowhere as dawn was breaking, not quite the man they wanted; but it was a step in the right direction.

Chip's eyes were glued to his binoculars studying the features of the old man they'd dumped out in the country; he was accompanied by two younger men, larger specimens' in fact very large thugs. Well thought Chip, the other villain must turn up now, perhaps not today but within the next few days. Chip murmured a few words aloud,

"It will be interesting to know how long these scum stay in the flat entertaining the whore, the old boy well; he is I think a very dangerous cold killer."

Then Chip sat in silence, glancing at his watch repeatedly wondering and waiting. Suddenly worrying about the safety of the girl, the monsters in his mind began creeping out of the shadows, regurgitating painful memories from the past; or were old wounds being ripped open! The old chap with his henchmen left the flat after three hours; seeing this scum leave the building made Chip's flesh creep, he felt everything wasn't right for the girl. Perhaps it was just an ex copper's nose telling him all was not right. For the moment Chip shrugged it off, after all, thought Chip I'll have to waken Pilgrim then we will be forced to enter the building ourselves.

Supposing I'm wrong? Our cover will be blown—then we'll be back where we started. Chip sat for a while contemplating, trying to deny the effort of visiting the flat opposite with all its inherent risks, placing with it all the faults and problems that could erupt by insisting on a quick call. Nevertheless Chip had this overwhelming urge to visit the establishment, he stood up then left his seat by the window to go into Pilgrim's room; he was fast asleep.

For a moment Chip stood motionless full of indecision, but suddenly his hand went out to Pilgrim's shoulder then shook it. His eyes flicked open instantly turning over to lie on his back, then eyeing Chip standing over him grunting at the same time,

"Is it my turn now?"

"Not really Pilgrim, it's just that I've got this overwhelming need to visit the whore over the road mate, but unfortunately its not how it sounds!"

Pilgrim sat up blinking trying to focus his eyes after being aroused from a deep sleep, Chip explained to Pilgrim about the visits by their old sparring partner, the old man who liked to dance barefoot on the motorway, remembering he was a very vicious individual, which gave him an uneasy feeling that something was really wrong. Pilgrim rubbed his hands over his face before answering his friend.

"Okay, if that's how you feel, let's do it, I'm taking my new toy." Chip shrugged his shoulders,

"That's alright with me—I'll take mine as well."

Ten minutes later the two inquisitors were climbing the uncarpeted stairs up to the prostitute's rooms, very gradually they could smell the cheap aroma of a whore's boudoir.

The front door to the apartment was wide open without a sound coming from inside the flat, the two unwanted visitors stood motionless, then silently but carefully taking their weapons from under their coats grasping them with both hands, and then when they were ready, they nodded to each other agreeing to enter the premises. Moving in a very stealthy manner they crept down the short unlit hallway, slowly pushing open the door to the living area; fully expecting a demanding voice from someone somewhere inside, to question their presence but none came!

They were not ready for what confronted them, the walls and furniture were splashed with blood; there before their eyes hanging from the light in the middle of the room was the naked body of the young prostitute.

What was once a pretty face was now distorted horrifically, showing the awful pain she must have suffered. Her body was slashed to pieces, her breasts had lost their nipples, still dripping with blood; added to that there was a long very deep cut from her mouth to her vagina, this gross act, this awful demonstration of inhumanity to a fellow human being was unforgivable even by the good Lord himself; the onlookers guessed this work had been effectively performed very slowly! To create as much pain as was inhumanly possible!

The slashed mutilated flesh still hanging open oozing copious amounts of blood, which was dripping down onto an elderly woman laying dead below her, it was obviously the whore's maid, her throat was also cut, her face hideously twisted. The blood from the hanging girl still dripping onto her face, creating a sight that would be unacceptable in the darkest of horror movies! Pilgrim moved closer to feel her body,

"Chip her body is still warm, the bastard has just finished!"

The floor was awash with blood; Chip and Pilgrim were frozen to the spot, stunned at the sight and for the moment lost for words. Until Chip whispered,

"Pilgrim this is not the place for us to be found, it's as if this place was visited by Satan!"

Pilgrim grimaced as he answered in a whispered voice,

"You don't have to tell me, let's get out of here."

The unwanted guests made for the door but suddenly stopped when they heard a voice call out in a soft English Northern brogue,

"Teresa—are you there?"

The sound of movement up the hallway brought the person closer to them as they stood like statues, weapons in their hands pointing in the direction of the inquiring voice; holding their breath—waiting for the person to appear framed in the doorway. Pilgrim sincerely hoped it was just the one individual, thinking if there was more than one it could turn into a fire fight; attracting the boys in blue! What a thought that was, with the girl hanging from the light with he and Chip armed as if they were going to war!

The seconds ticked away like hours—suddenly he was there, fortunately standing alone, at first he never saw either of them; his eyes staring glued in horror at the suspended butchered naked body—that once was his lovely sister Teresa. His cold blues eyes flitted from the hanging horror, to rest on the two strangers confronting him; seismic shock waves still shaking his mind and body at the sight of his next of kin, causing him to produce a hoarse whisper as he asked the ultimate question,

"Eh lad who would do such a thing to such a harmless beautiful creature, did you commit this heinous crime?"

Chip answered this poignant question quietly and decisively,

"We are not capable of committing such an outrage to a fellow human being, but we know who did—that's for sure."

It was very impressing the way the young man was so cool, although confronted by this appalling sight of his beloved sister, tortured and butchered hanging from the light like a carcass of beef. Apart from the colour draining from his face, he never showed any feelings at all, but still managed to subdue mammoth personal pain, he was not only asking leading questions, but to directly concern himself about self survival in the face of unknown warriors. As witnesses to this, Pilgrim and Chip well—they in an unspoken way could only admire such astounding resilience!

The young man with the soft northern accent with blonde hair and a tan that looked perhaps it belonged to a country like Morocco; stood studying them for a few more seconds before speaking again. Once more the two men pointing their weapons against him realised this pause, was required by this sadly haunted individual to control his composure.

A brother who really wanted to lift his Teresa down from the vicious butcher's hook jutting through her skin, then hold her close and allow his teardrops to wash away her wounds, then to plead her forgiveness among his tears for allowing himself to entice her into his evil schemes. But he did neither; only pulled himself together with an iron will, to pose the all important question, the only giveaway was the sudden jutting of a square chin, emanating total aggression, donned like an actors prop!

"Well—what the hell do you intend doing with me now lad?"

He fired this question at them as if his tongue was a machine gun, hesitated then proceeded,

"I was told you were after me—I just could not work out why. It was not as if I knew you, I was certain you were not a political enemy. You were never a target at any time for me, so what the hell do you two toss-pots want?"

Pilgrim answered this time, addressing this fellow professional in a quiet voice; but speaking with a quiet clarity with firm emphasis,

"I would like you first to observe very carefully the weapons we hold in our hands, just in case you might think our concentration may waver enough during your small talk; so that we lose our awareness, possibly convincing you to risk taking a shot then running for it. Please do not even think about it—because it will cost you your life—we are not amateurs.

My colleague and I do not know you, we bear you no malice and we offer you our sincere sympathy, not any of God's creature's humans or animals should meet their end in such a manner! Also I would like to add we have watched this place for several days, so we know for certain who is responsible for these brutal killings; it is just very sad that we arrived too late. You must know the murderer he's on your team, the old boy, well spoken—dresses like a city gent."

He nodded then responded, answering in his soft northern accent but with a resonance of venom,

"I know well to whom you're referring lad, and I must say it looks like his handy work, if I ever get the opportunity I will manufacture a fitting end for such a sick old man. What I would like to know directly—exactly where do we go from here? For it looks as if you have the advantage: that is at the moment."

The last few words slightly amused Chip and Pilgrim, in lighter circumstances they would have laughed openly but, Pilgrim spoke in a sombre note.

"That's a good question along with a fair assumption of the situation, what do you think our next move should be Pilgrim?"

"Chip—I am going to ask him to first place both his hands on his head very slowly and very carefully, then take two sideways paces to your right which will take you away from the door, then turn around to face the wall which will then be behind you, if you don't want to join your sister, do what you're told to do. Otherwise this machine pistol will cut you in half and I'm eager to use it, as I'm sure you know it's an extremely efficient weapon."

The captured assassin did exactly as he was asked with no fuss; Chip took from his pocket a pair of handcuffs while Pilgrim took no chances, he stood with the pistol's barrel against the assassin's head.

Chip pulled the killers jacket off to pull his arms around to his back, he then expertly snapped police bracelets around his wrists, then carefully draped the jacket around his shoulders; to hide his inhibited state.

"Now gentleman, I think we'd better get away from this awful scene as quickly as possible. As for you friend—I'm sorry that the young lady fell victim to such a monster, also I'm so disappointed we did not decide to call in here earlier, a life could have been saved by perhaps fifteen minutes."

Chip paused for a second to shake his head in sadness for that was not to be—then spoke quickly and decisively,

"Come on let's go."

The handcuffed man never spoke a word as they quickly walked him across the street, then up to their flat.

"There is one decent act we can perform for the young lady, and that is to notify the police of her body hanging there, you can't do it! You're a wanted man."

Pilgrim grimaced at the thought of the body hanging for a couple of days, adding,

"Yes that's what I'll do!"

The hostage stood sullenly watching them as they cleaned their own flat of fingerprints and all personal effects, this process took an hour; till at last they were ready to leave the premises. Pilgrim waited while Chip fetched the car to the street below, on the honk of the horn Pilgrim marched the hostage down the stairs then out into the street into the waiting car.

Pilgrim sat in the back with the handcuffed man while Chip did the driving; Chip after buckling up his seat belt turned to consult Pilgrim on their next move.

"I suppose we're taking Moses here back to the mansion?"

"Absolutely correct Chip, the only point that bothers me that it's a fair bet he'll want us to return under the cover of darkness. Hanging onto this man handcuffed for too long is a problem; even now—he should be released."

"Hmm it's a problem alright!"

Chip reached over to a holdall on the backseat and unzipped it; he then reached inside taking from it a roll of wide black adhesive tape perfect for their needs.

"This stuff will do the trick; I'll tape him up while you cover him."

Pilgrim held his pistol to the hostage's head while Chip taped him from his shoulders to his wrists taking the tape all around the car seat, then again draped his jacket around his shoulders so that it completely hid the binding. Chip made a point of warning the hostage!

"Now listen, I won't tape your mouth but if you attempt to draw attention to yourself, you will get a bonus whack on the head from my friend in the back. Then—you will definitely spend the rest of the journey in the boot with your mouth taped up, and no food, do you understand that?"

Moses nodded very slowly with hate showing in his eyes.

"Good, but I'm telling you right now—I'll kill you in a blink of an eyelid if I have to, for if that's how you neglect your sister, you aren't much of a man that would be missed by the rest of the human race." Chip was still burning from the sight of the young girl hanging from the light. Pilgrim was also starting to get impatient, mainly because he was hungry and tired Chip sensed his condition, so he strove to calm and reassure him.

"Chip don't worry about him, I'll be pleased to blow his head off if he makes one wrong move."

The car stopped in a quiet cul-de-sac, while Pilgrim fetched three bags of fried potato chips from a nearby fish and chip shop; then they released the prisoner's arms from his elbows down. That just allowed him to eat his food, they ate in silence, Moses could not stop casting quick side glances at the man next to him, desperately attempting to work out any means of escape; unfortunately he knew he was dealing with two very good professionals.

When they were all finished eating, he was re-taped securely. The evening shadows were lengthening, so they decided to start their journey to the mansion without phoning to warn Tobias of their arrival; appreciating the danger of the informer at the mansion, who might very well cause further problems.

On the journey the men fell silent; Chip opened the window enjoying the rush of fresh air, hoping it would stop him falling asleep; for the road out in front of him lit up by his headlights stretched out like a hypnotizing yellow incandescent ribbon. Also praying the fresh air would clear his brain of the sight he just could not get out of his head, the picture of the prostitute hanging from the ceiling with the open wounds all over her body.

What a pretty girl she was, and how she must have been at one time such a picture when she was five years of age, no doubt the apple of her father's eye, what an awful waste of a life. Pilgrim nudged his driver to bring him back from his troubled thoughts,

"Hey Chip you've suddenly gone very quiet what's the problem?" Chip never answered right away, but took several moments to drag his mind back from the past,

"Seeing that young girl brought back all the wrong memories Pilgrim!"

"Why don't you tell me about it then? I'd love to know."

"The story's easy to tell, it was the smell of the place; the cheap perfume."

For that moment in time Chip's thoughts were way back in the past, so then once more he cleared his throat with his mind to carry on talking.

"I was unfortunate to fall in love with a lady of the night when I was on the drug squad, strangely enough she was also blonde and petite. I managed to get her away from the business if you can call it that, fixed her up to live at a decent address, surrounded by a decent people.

The pimp, who always boasted he owned her, searched and searched until he found his so called property then strangled the life out of her. I found her the same way we found that young girl back there."

"Did you find the pimp Chip?"

"Oh yes I found him alright, after finding the girl carved up and strangled; I then forgot all about going to work—a sort of madness came over me. I also searched and searched combing the underworld in London, finding an informant that with a little persuasion told me the whereabouts of this animal. I eventually found him in Liverpool after a tip off; I beat him to death, simple as that! Amazingly I managed to just get off with a manslaughter charge."

"That was lucky! Mind you I didn't think you had it in you?"

"Neither did I, a deep anger takes over your life—not a shouting anger, an anger that boils and boils deep down, of course when you find the culprit who is the cause of your torment, you turn into a madman—sadly there's no way back! I'm not proud of the event, in fact I'm really ashamed; but there you are it happened and there is nothing I can do about it now.

You know the worse thing about it all, was having to explain the entire episode to my wife Jean, who I'd been with for five years. I put myself in the position of having explaining it all to her prior to entering the courtroom."

Pilgrim was really spellbound by this tale of love and violence, curious to know his wife's answer,

"Whatever did she say?"

"She never said a word Pilgrim—just turned on her heels and walked out of the building and out of my life; I've never seen her since that awful day!"

"That's quite a story. Chip I've got to ask you this—I would really like to know, how did you get the name Chip?"

"Pilgrim if you had my name—you would have called yourself Chip!"

"Well come on tell me your real name."

"I tell you what Pilgrim only two other people know my real name and they are my sister and my ex-wife, if I tell you, promise not to laugh!"

"As if I would Chip, come on—I'm dying to know."

Poor Chip heaved a huge sigh then began to relate the story of his name,

"When I got married the choir boy couldn't stop giggling when the vicar asked, will you Horace Arnold Whittaker take this woman for your wife? Or something like that. The little sod giggled all through the ceremony."

Pilgrim laughed,

"It's not as bad as all that it could have been Sue as in the song, I remember when I was in prison with you, I always wanted to know the answer to that. I promise I won't say anything more about it."

Nobody spoke for a few miles then their hostage broke the silence,

"I'd like to know why you are taking me to the mansion?"

Pilgrim resented talking to the fascist but answered him just the same,

"The answer to that is easy, because we get a bonus for taking you, that's why we were hired; just to catch you then take you to the hall."

Then the killer smiled as he spoke,

"I'll tell you something, you want to hope and pray they kill me, for if they don't it will be my turn to hunt you down, and when I do I'll kill you that's for sure."

Pilgrim thought for a few moments before answering,

"You know bastards like you have been trying to kill me for years, especially young prats like you, after what I've just seen you want to hope and pray I don't come looking for you!"

The rest of the journey was spent in silence; Pilgrim's anger subsided not wanting to upset the fact the prat was wanted alive at the mansion. So he filled his mind with the thought of the lovely lolly that was on offer for a job completed; the assassin was the man to break the silence,

"Do you know what these people are after, have you any idea what it is?

Pilgrim hesitated before he answered,

"No we haven't a clue, we were just called in to do a job, so—after we're paid we don't really care what they're after."

Again the car fell into silence before the alien passenger pursued the answer to the question he'd just asked,

"I can tell you what it is, the most valuable article in the world. It is the Holy Grail, something they will kill and slaughter to get at any cost."

Chip was quick to answer this time.

"The Holy Grail! What value would that be to an ordinary person; surely it only holds value to the clergy or the establishment of the church."

The killer was quick to answer,

"Oh yes that's exactly how the ordinary man in the street thinks, but to certain characters it holds mystic powers, that can be what ever you want it to be. So you have all these different voyeurs from ambiguous backgrounds searching for this valuable relic from the past."

"That's a bit vague, using words like ambiguous to describe the situation, come on give it out a bit clearer."

The orator half turned his head to speak to Pilgrim,

"Well—I said that because if I told you what it really meant you would most likely laugh at the reality."

Chip smiled at the hostage's words as he spoke,

"Give it a try, the worse thing we can do is laugh, and let's face it we can always do with a laugh."

The northerner's face hardened at the sarcastic remark from Pilgrim, but he resumed speaking anyway,

"The persons I'm referring to as ambiguous are the people from the dark side, those who practice in the black art. The point is we cannot even start to know how dangerous these people are, to us the uninitiated—it seems a load of old bollocks; unfortunately it really is a way of life to them.

As for being evil they enjoy slicing a piece off of the policies invented by the Devil.

You both witnessed some of their work performed on my sister, sure I've killed—many times but not to the evil depths that these animals sink to. I know exactly what their plans are to extract the truth from me to get their grimy hands on the Holy Grail, what happened to my sister will happen to me and if you're not careful it will happen to you."

These far fetched sounding statements from the young assassin would in certain circumstances be laughed at, but bearing in mind the outrageous payments for their services plus the killing just witnessed by Pilgrim and Chip; plus the temple Pilgrim stumbled into made the words of their hostage ring true. It left the two boys without words to sum up the situation, a silence the soft spoken Yorkshire man was quick to exploit!

"So lads, you seem to have gone very quiet, has the truth of the situation become too much for you to accept?"

Chip cleared his throat to speak first,

"The first question I must ask is do you know where and who possesses the Holy Grail? For from what you've just told us, it is something you will be forced to tell these people what they want anyway."

Again silence reigned for several minutes until the captive answered,

"I have become aware as to why they sent you after me, I did originally manage to get my hands on this precious article, I stole it from an antique dealer in Surrey. Again I just passed it on to the person who was employing me, at the time I never dreamt in my wildest dreams the value, that these Satan's people placed on the article concerned."

Chip was quick to answer this time,

"It all seems very sinister to me—but I must say certain things do add up, the cloak of secrecy that has hidden from us the real reasons why we are being paid to do the job at all; also where do we go from here?"

"Wait a minute."

Said Pilgrim very quickly,

"We can't take too much notice of him, he is looking after his own selfish needs, I think all we can do is deliver this man as we agreed, then stay to see what happens. If we think he faces any physical abuse well—perhaps we will have to think again."

Chip just nodded, it was all becoming very heavy going, so he settled into his own thoughts.

The car turned left off the main road into the driveway of the mansion, passing through the open high ornamental wrought iron gates; that introduced the ride down the long drive. As Chip drove he could not help his thoughts slipping back to his relationship with the lady of the night—that he loved so much, and then his mind traversed the chain of events right up to the killing of the hostage's sister; then the talk about Holy Grail. Thinking to himself, I do sometimes wonder if the Grail is symbolic to anything that is precious to any individual; again the affair with the lady of the night and then his imprisonment sprung into his mind!

How the experience changed him as a man, the violence, the killing and the sordid necessity of having to mix with such low life he never knew could ever exist. Then the grand finale, the trial—phew! I was lucky to get away with five years imprisonment. The other cons could hardly wait to lay their hands on an ex CID police officer, Chip was always handy with his fists; which as it turned out it was just as well.

His parents could not help noticing how the escapade had changed him, while his mother said nothing, his father was quick to voice his opinion warning him against being to harsh on the world, in other words telling him to water down his wallowing in bitterness; otherwise it would destroy him!

Well Chip thought—I wonder how much all this brutality will affect Pilgrim and me; as for the Yorkshire lad what an impact the death of his sister must have had on him; all this must affect a person's thinking!

The car stopped beneath the highly decorative stone portico which sheltered the grand sweeping elegantly shaped granite steps, which led up to the front door of the mansion. In precise timing as the car stopped, the front door opened then the butler with the flattened nose and posh accent hurried down the steps to take the hostage from them as Chip whispered,

"Pilgrim I think we were watched all the way down the drive on closed circuit television."

Pilgrim answered in a quiet tone of voice,

"I'm sure you're right."

The tape was cut from around the front seat while Pilgrim held the gun to the head of the unfortunate; when free he was quickly handcuffed then whisked away up the stairs, then lost in the vastness of the rambling Victorian labyrinth.

Pilgrim and Chip were met by the man in the wheelchair, Tobias as he called himself; greeted them like long lost sons, which made Chip and Pilgrim feel very suspicious and of course dreadfully insecure, feeling their weapons in their pockets making sure they were very ready to their hands.

As the evening progressed they wondered, whether or not if they were being a little unfair, but forewarned with the extra information they had gathered from the fascist, felt their attitude was justifiable, and no doubt would be rewarded before the evening was over.

The two conquering heroes ate a good meal at the same table as their host, Tobias, with the flat nosed butler hovering in the background. When the food was eaten, followed by the table being cleared, their host Tobias suddenly tired of small talk; he then moved the conversation onto more significant discussions.

"You two have exceeded my wildest dreams; I must admit I didn't think you'd last five minutes. To do what you did to survive then win, was a truly brilliant performance, there's no doubt you've earned the money you were promised; I'm pleased to inform you the money was paid into your accounts late this afternoon.

If I remember right the promised sum was half a million each, so that was the amount deposited in your names; I hope you are both happy with that!"

Pilgrim and Chip looked at each other in amazement.

"How did you know our account numbers or where we bank, are you clairvoyant?"

Tobias smiles at the boy's remarks along with the surprised looks on their faces, answering with his cultured words,

"Please don't worry about such trivialities; you must remember I am a man of outstanding substance and not without an extensive knowledge of the world that surrounds me. Now you must listen, because I would like to move onto more important details, the question is whether or not you wish to continue with this quest on my behalf; bearing in mind that to accept another mission would bring you higher rewards."

Pilgrim leaned forward in his seat on hearing these words.

"I suppose it means greater risks than we've just experienced?"

Tobias stretched and arched his back in his chair closing his eyes as he did, he opened them then resumed speaking,

"Please excuse me, sitting in this chair all day makes my back ache, I dream of the day when I'll have a chance to walk again but who knows. Still I digress, the risks you speak of will be no greater than the ones you've already endured, with the techniques you use—you would be foolish not to accept my offer."

Chip spoke slowly in a low voice,

"What would be on offer for such an adventure?"

Tobias's face split into a grin as he spoke.

"That's what I like to hear words like adventure, shows you have the right spirit for the Oddesy on offer. I tell you what's on the table or better—in your bank, a million pounds each paid into any bank of anywhere in the world of your choosing."

The two proposed adventurers, for a moment were stunned at such a financial gesture; they cast a glance at each other before turning their gaze once more to the face of the man who just made this astonishing proposal. Chip cleared his throat before speaking,

"You must be a desperate man to get hold of whatever it is you're after!"

Again Tobias straightened his back putting a grimace on his face as he did so answering,

"You're absolutely correct; there is something I'm desperate to own, desperate to hold it in my hand, so because of that desperation; quite willing to pay the right price it demands. I also think you two are the men to get it for me, in fact if you are able to acquire it quicker than I expect, then I will pay a bonus on top of the sum I have already mentioned. I can't give more incentive than that."

Pilgrim laughed,

"As they say in the movies it's an offer we can't refuse, I'm sure we both accept your offer."

"Good—very good." Tobias smiled rubbing his hands looking convincingly like Scrooge knowing Christmas was cancelled. The flat nosed butler appeared to open the double doors to the spacious dining room, then stood holding the handles of the wheelchair waiting for the order from Tobias to push him out of the room; but Tobias spoke to them once more,

"In the morning you will find at your bedside after breakfast the details you will need to resume your quest."

The invalid then held up his finger, which was the order for old flat nose to immediately pull him away from the table and out of the room. Just as Tobias was leaving, he gave the order for the butler to stop; he turned to address the mercenaries once more.

"Very shortly my butler will return to show you to your rooms for the night, I'm sure you both must be very tired, if you need any tea you only have to ask; then it will be brought up to your rooms."

It was Chip's turn to answer,

"Thank you, it would be nice to retire with a good cup of tea."

Pilgrim muttered under his breath,

"Yeah bloody wonderful."

The doors closed, once more they were on their own, for a few seconds they were immersed in silence until Chip smiled and broke it.

"What a turn up for the books, what do you make of it Pilgrim."

I'm like you stunned; then again I wonder what's in store for us. Also are we going to look for the golden chalice, or as the Paddy called it the Holy Grail, it's still all shrouded in mystery."

As Pilgrim finished speaking the doors opened again then flat nose entered, addressing them in his usual curt well spoken manner.

"Would you please follow me?"

Both of them did just that, they climbed the beautiful staircase, to the second floor this time; too adjacent rooms in the shadowy corridor. Their room was the same lay out as the last one they slept in with the secondary lighting, which threw deep shadows into the corners of the room. Pilgrim had a quick look round before going to the room next door where Chip was, Chip was sitting on the bed waiting for Pilgrim speaking to him as he entered,

"How are we going to shape up tonight? Let's face it we have to remember our captured gun for hire is in the house somewhere, we really don't know how competent these thugs are. They might be a right load of idiots for all we know."

Pilgrim smiled as he spoke;

"I think you're right, if that little prat manages to do a Houdini then he'll most certainly come looking for us. So we'll revert to our usual style keeping guard while one sleeps okay. Bearing in mind you drove us here I'll take the first watch."

"Fine by me Pilgrim, but tell me, why I do get the feeling we are being watched all the time."

Chip stood up, switched the lighting right up to allow them to see clearly, then started to walk around the room looking for anything that looked like a camera; Pilgrim joined in doing the same thing. For about five minutes they both walked around the room scrutinising the ceiling, also the pictures on the wall. Until Chip found what he was looking for, a very small lens peeking out from an oil painting hung at the end of the room facing the bed.

Chip walked over to the side of his bed picking up his holdall, taking from it the roll of tape which was used to keep the hostage under control. He then went over to the picture, tore a small piece of tape from the reel, and then deftly stuck it over the tiny lens living in the corner of the oil painting.

"I dunno about you matey but I'm shattered, so I'll crawl into the pit right now then shower in the morning; if that's alright with you?"

Pilgrim nodded,

"Certainly, get to bed but do our usual tricks, sleep on the floor on the opposite side of the bed to the door; then we'll tuck up pillows into the bed to look as if you're in there. That way you draw the fire but remain in a safe place. I'll be over there on that chair watching the door. Have no fear I'll call you at three, let's hope it will be no sooner. You never know perhaps old Tobias has ambitions to rid himself of us, we're certainly sailing in strange waters!"

Chip agreed and was soon stripped to his underwear, tucked up in a bed on the floor snoring, while his partner in this war of survival did as he said he was going to do.

Pilgrim switched the lighting to its secondary stage then sat on the chair in a dark corner of the room which the lighting created, with his automatic very handy. Fortunately managing to find a couple of magazines in the paper rack by the dressing table, he flicked through the pages finding something to read which would pass the long hours of the night.

Unfortunately for him being only human, it was at times like this other visitors came flying in with the shadows in the darkened corners all from his past, time to dwell on the certain moments in his life that he'd been warned not to do. Pilgrim thought of things he wish he'd done and many things he wished he hadn't.

He smiled to himself when he thought about Julie; at least he was feeling a bit better about his life. I really would like to see her, but not at this particular time it might get her all caught up like the Paddy's sister; I'm finding it difficult forgetting what happened to her.

He made himself think about his children, he really missed them, it was so painful being away from them for so long. Under normal circumstances I would be able to phone them, but this situation is far from normal. A few times Pilgrim sat up to listen intently, as he heard footsteps in the corridor outside his room, but they passed by.

Whatever are we going to do about the bastard who committed that evil act on the prostitute? Are we going to pretend we didn't see anything? Pilgrim wondered if he and Chip would ever be able to disentangle themselves from these villains from either side.

One, do we know too much, as for the other side well perhaps they won't be happy until we are in the ground full of bullets; a tricky problem. As I've said to myself before only time will tell.

What am I going to do about the two men who put me away for several years? I really need to contact a friend of mine who's still working within the busy labyrinths of the M I 6 head quarters. I'm sure he will be able to tell me everything I want to know, if and when we are free from for this mausoleum I'll be able to speak to him; I just have to hope he's available. Pilgrim's duty watch was uneventful along with Chip's.

CHAPTER 9
He Never Knew!

The hostage sat in chains manacled against the wall at the end of the temple, next to what looked like an altar for dubious anti Christ activities; at exactly the same spot Pilgrim surveyed when he went on his night time prowl. The existing excessive splashes of old blood stains on the floor, which were also spattered across the wood panelling lining the wall behind him; had been fearfully noted by the newcomer.

The unhappy guest tried to peer into the semi darkness through eyes partially closed; due to the heavy punching plus the kicking he received as a bonus from his benevolent interrogators. The durable Assassin sat there trying to take stock of his position, aware of the fact that because he was still conscious after such a beating, it just might give him an advantage, albeit a small one; but nevertheless still an advantage!

Fortunately he heard the old man in the wheelchair give the order that he did not want the fascist to die, so he was expecting some food to arrive at any time. Gradually his eyes were focusing to see his abysmal surroundings, he wondered what his old priest who used to train him for the choir; who also used him as an altar boy because of his angelic features; would make of this situation. I'm sure he would have said,

"It's the Devil's abode, and these are Satan's people!"

In his thick Yorkshire accent; Moses muttered in a loud voice,

"I know he would be right."

Moses cursed himself for talking aloud, so he demanded from his battered brain a higher level of concentration to solve his present predicament, ignoring the aches and the pains of the bruises. Thinking only of the necessity to escape then defeat this anti Christ enemy, if—Moses thought. If—I could manage to get a scissors grip on the legs of the flat nosed posh speaking character who acted as the butler to the wheel bound boss; I'd stand a chance.

The damaged assassin let his hands hang loose as if they were lifeless, then he hung his head in the same way, thinking; now that really looks fatal. Then he drew his legs up against his body as tight as he could, hoping he could reach a small knife tucked away in his socks; but he couldn't.

So he tried to lay as flat as he could on his back to push his legs into the air, then bending both legs as tight as he could to his chest; allowing his hands to reach into his sock, only then could he just reach the knife.

After all this effort he was red faced and breathless, which forced him to grab a few moments to rest sitting there with the knife in his hand, but not wanting to wast any more time—so after a few moments passed, he wriggled about trying to drop the knife down his sleeve; which he succeeded in doing.

The exertion coupled with the pain of moving his badly beaten body, had exhausted his reserves, so he decided to rest, Moses slumped against the wall; allowing his head with his hands to slump in the same way. What exactly he could do with the knife down his sleeve Moses didn't know, but—he thought you never know; hope in these extreme situations must always spring eternal.

Let's face it Moses thought, you never know the mug might release one hand to let me eat, that's all I want one hand then he's dead. The thought of slamming the knife into one of his main interrogator's, gave him a very warm feeling; which might just help to make this awful headache go away.

Several hours passed before he heard the heavy steps of the flat nosed butler, followed by the turn of the key in the lock, unfortunately in the half light he could only take a quick glance at the approaching corpulent figure, then closed his eyes to resume his hanging appearance; but he could hear the thug's footsteps getting nearer and nearer.

Moses let his head hang along with his hands, also letting his body slump, with the bruised swollen features plus the blood splashed across his face; he knew he must have looked a sorry sight to his jailer.

The hired hand stood for a moment undecided what to do, flat nose put the tray down on the floor then knelt in front of the prisoner; muttering to himself. He knew the job he had was very difficult, the servant thug was an informant working for the bulbous headed ugly bastard; he was going to some how free this fugitive; then make it look as if he was the damaged party.

He once again studied the sad blooded figure chained to the wall, with his head and hands suspended by the manacles. The observer shuddered at the sight of the young man embraced in the gloomy surroundings of this Satan's temple.

Then the man who was a double agent very carefully took a key from his pocket, as he moved closer then started to unlock the right hand manacle! The thespian like captive could never have known this strutting perfunctory pretender was his friend; and he was about to set him free!

Unfortunately for this ambiguous hireling, Moses could not believe his luck, the time from when the man took the key from his pocket to put it into the lock seemed an age; at last Moses heard the click of the lock then felt the manacle drop from his wrist.

Paddy's hand dropped lifeless to the floor, as Moses slowly lifted his head to see the butler turn to reach for the tray of food. In that very instant Moses struck like a cobra, the small five inch blade was buried into the neck of his jailer.

The butler keeled over towards his assailant; Moses never let it go at that! He plunged the knife into the neck of the man again and again and again, until he was totally silent; not even a gurgling sound came from the butchered blooded body.

Moses then quickly as he could struggled to drag the bloody torso closer to him, enabling him to go through his pockets to find the key. In seconds Moses was at the door peering down the corridor, revitalised at the unexpected thought of freedom; along with a very satisfying feeling that he'd wreaked revenge on at least one of his torturers.

The future now looked even brighter; perhaps he could add to his score, and kill the two men who were responsible for bringing him here, he changed his mind deciding to escape from these Satan's people; but first succumbed to the attraction of thumbing through files he stumbled on in a small side room!

Moses scrambled across open countryside in the pitch black, falling into water filled ditches then wading through long wet grass. After a couple of hours dawn started to break, hoping he'd managed to put several miles between him and the mansion.

He decided to sit and enjoy a well-earned rest on a wet grassy bank; planning what was to be done next, first I'll have to get back to my flat in London. He took off one shoe and sock then fiddled about with his fingers; pulling out a stolen credit card that would serve to pay the bills for food and transport back to his flat. This man was trained to survive, no matter what conditions surrounded him!

Just for a moment, that fleeting second; the smell of the open countryside, his wet feet and socks; brought back the memories of his childhood, he could almost hear the sound of Teresa's mischievous tinkling little girls laughter. Both children neglected by unhappy parents, making sure the children were tucked away from their responsibilities, in to some other's even less caring institution!

How we both adored the dash to freedom from the convent school, playing truant regularly when he and his sister were children. Teresa was so comical impersonating the different teachers at the school, causing them both to fall over convulsed with laughter; such happy days snatched from the poverty and misery that surrounded them.

Tears began to roll down his face, now the full force of her death was starting to hit him like a hammer blow; suddenly these happy moments from the past were framed in an inky blackness.

Her loyal ubiquitous love ripped away by an act of heinous violence for no good reason, she knew nothing. Now he was alone he realised how much he had adored his pretty sister; knowing from this moment on how much he was going to miss her.

The born again killer within him pushed aside the sentimentality, to deal with the present. Moses could not resist letting his mind wander back over the last few hours. How lucky he was to stumble across the room containing the old style filing cabinets holding the complete details of the two men he wanted so badly.

Before he planned their disposal, there are four evil characters, still walking around free and unpunished, that needed to be brought to heel; the deadly group of killers responsible for the outrageous torture and butchery of my beloved Teresa!

Moses with his sister were raised and educated within the strict confines of the Catholic Church. This background of poverty, coupled with the strict discipline enforced by the harshness of unfeeling authority was thrust upon them; it conceived to breed a package situation that helped to twist the young minds onto paths, that in their straight-laced communities would be called; the road to Satan's arms.

When Moses came of age he also joined the Patriotic British Party, with all its iron principles and innate violence; while Teresa—well she sold the only thing she had ever owned. Trading her wares first in the darker labyrinths of northern cities, then to London; struggling at first to survive against threats and acts of violence from the local villains in Soho.

As always in her life, Moses quickly came to the rescue, crushing any opposition by giving protection British Patriotic Party style. All these thoughts from the past rushed through his mind.

After all that, the poverty and destitution coupled with the bitter acceptance of Teresa's decision to turn to prostitution as a way of earning her living; was an awful situation but he learned to accept her status in life, even though at the time it really hurt him!

For his sister Teresa to end up hanging from a light fitting in a seedy Soho flat, butchered like a side of pork was not an acceptable way for his sister to die. Revenge! Revenge! Revenge! At this moment in his life was foremost in his mind.

He sat on the wet bank for a little while longer, how he dreamed when he realised the true value of the chalice. The million pounds was for him with Teresa to escape the gutters of London, hopefully running to the sunlight of freedom in happy exile to the Americas.

That dream was now gone, in its place a nightmare ending for his sister, someone had to pay for destroying a vision, he knew exactly who was going to receive the bill. Wet through and very cold he managed to find an older car to hot wire, tucked away in a back alley of a small village, in his scramble to escape.

Filling it with petrol using the stolen credit card, he made his way to London; dumping the car several miles from his home, going by black cab the last few miles. Moses' small flat enveloped him as an embracing woman offering warmth, hot water food and rest, for his bruised bones and empty stomach.

The minor luxuries massaged his brain to concoct a fitting end for all his enemies, Moses made a cup of tea then dosed it with a dash of whisky. He picked up his tea as he settled into his settee, pulling over a small coffee table to place his feet on and relaxed to give himself time to think. Musing aloud,

"Of course capturing the girl will not be a problem. The other four that's going to be difficult."

Then with a cheeky grin through the bruises, added to himself,

"But I'll do it!"

* * *

At seven in the morning they were both showered and dressed sitting in the dining room, ready for their breakfast. They were joined by Tobias with all the obligatory small talk, which seemed too civilised bearing in mind the company they were in.

The boys enjoyed a good breakfast, in fact as Pilgrim said it seemed ages since they were able to act in such a relaxed manner. When the breakfast was finished, Tobias pushed his plate away from him; then looked across the table at the two men he'd decided to pin his hopes on.

"As I said last night every thing you require is on your bedside table, at this point I bid you well and wish you all the luck you need. I hope you come back with the article I've searched for all my life."

The man was true to his word, instructions to give them an address, names and extravagant expenses were where Tobias said they would be. Pilgrim with Chip set out that morning unsure of their future and feeling very insecure, a feeling that was going to keep them alive with a bit of luck. Chip was driving once again and he stopped half way up the drive causing Pilgrim to suddenly look concerned,

"What's up Chip what have you stopped for?"

"We are a pair of fools we never asked what happened to the man called Moses. I've a good mind to go back and find out!"

"Oh don't do that Chip—fuck that killer—forget him no doubt we'll run across him again; even if we do I'm sure we'll have to kill him."

"You know Pilgrim we are getting as bad as them, just having to stay alive makes us as violent as them."

"Chip I know you're right but we took the job on and that's the end of it, let's look forward to checking out the antique shop along with the owner in the Portobello road."

Chip nodded then fell silent, squeezing the accelerator along with his conscience!

CHAPTER 10
An Old Flame Warms a Cold Heart

Julie sat in front of the dressing table mirror deep in thought; she missed seeing her brother Chip; it was two months, since he left to see this strange character about a mysterious offer of work. Of course the interesting bit was, he was also going to see the love of her life big tasty Pilgrim, well Julie thought I've not seen hide nor hair of either of them; it's a bit worrying.

Julie picked up the comb to groom her long blonde hair, that tumbled down on to her shoulders then turned up into pretty ringlets, her blue eyes were so deep a man could swim in them; matching the pale complexion in which they were set. The ladies figure was trim her legs shapely and very long; all this feminine artillery was accompanied by an intelligent inquisitive brain.

Thoughts about her brother tumbled cross her mind—I'm sure I have Chip's mobile number somewhere; the trouble is he changed his number so many times when he was in the police force I got out of the habit of keeping it. It was Saturday, all the week Julie had been looking forward to treating herself to something new, you never know she thought Pilgrim just might pop in out of the blue.

The phone rang on the table next to her, so she picked it up almost immediately hoping it was her brother. She was greeted by a male voice with a very friendly soft Yorkshire accent asking,

"Is that Chip's sister? You sound just like he said you would."

For a moment Julie was caught wrong footed, talking to somebody who knew of her when she didn't know them.

"Well actually yes it is, obviously you know Chip, do you know where he is? I haven't seen him for ages."

"Yes I was with him about a week ago he asked me to give you a call, also to give you his kind regard; but to stress you are not to worry."

Julie was very pleased with this information; the good news encouraged her to be more overt with this strange voice that was getting friendlier by the second.

"How was Pilgrim, he is all right is he still with Chip?"

"Oh yes Pilgrim's still with him, a real nice guy. I got on with him really well, he sends his love and expects to see you soon, perhaps we can meet somewhere for a meal; your brother said to look after you."

Julie hesitated,

"Well that's really nice of you but—I don't know if I should, after all I really don't know you."

"I understand Julie, I'll tell you what just to prove to you that I'm a close friend; I'll give you a name only two other people in this world know—that is his ex-wife Jean and you. Are you ready for this,—the name is "Horace." I got it out of him when we spent a night having a few drinks."

Julie couldn't stop laughing.

"You must be a very good friend, he really hates that name, okay call me later in the week."

The assassin mentally panicked, he knew the sooner he met the girl the better chance he had of getting hold of her, in case the brother turned up on the scene. So he quickly made an earlier offer for a dinner date,

"Well I can't make it later in the week, I know—how about Monday evening, I'll pick you up at your place; we'll have a meal or something."

Julie hesitated for a second—then thought to hell with it; I'll take a chance on what he looks like.

"Okay Monday eight-o-clock, I'll look forward to it"

"That's good Julie I'm sure you won't regret it—we'll have a fine evening."

The Northerner put the phone down wearing a grin from ear to ear, as he moved out of the phone box he accidentally bumped into a parked bicycle.

The handlebars catching him in the ribs ordinarily he would not have noticed the bump; but after the beating he took at the house, he felt every light touch; it really caused him to groan.

He was pleased that he managed to kill the well spoken flat nosed butler in his scamper for freedom from the Victorian mansion; Moses could not believe what a bit of luck it was running into the room where all the personal files were kept; now he badly wanted the two smart arses Pilgrim and Chip.

He was very near to possessing the one valuable possession that would bring the two men to heel. Moses returned to his flat feeling very pleased that the first part of his plan was beginning to work.

He paced the room for about fifteen minutes, and then suddenly made up his mind to do it; he picked up the phone, after dialling a cultured voice answered the call. It was Harrison the bulbous headed ugly bastard, Moses swallowed hard replying,

"This is Moses I want to do a deal."

The phone went dead for a moment, Moses could sense Harrison was thinking as quickly as he could, he answered in a tone with a style that shrieked of suspicion,

"Explain to me what sort of deal—supposing I agree—where do we meet? Not I hope in that smelly bar as before!"

Moses answered quickly and persuasively as he could,

"No of course not, as for the deal well we originally agreed to half a million pounds cash, and no messing about, cash!"

Again a pause before Harrison answered,

"Okay it's a deal, but first where do we meet before I agree?"

Moses was now smiling,

"We'll keep the meeting simple, I thought in a public place for it's just a matter of swapping parcels. There is a narrow street at the bottom of Hampstead Hill West, its called Damask Street; we can meet tonight at seven." Harrison cleared his throat,

"Okay let's do it, one small point—will you be alone or will you have your sister with you?"

Moses' stomach tightened then turned over, knowing exactly what Harrison was doing, trying to find out whether or not he knew his sister had been murdered. He screwed down the sickness that suddenly entered his stomach, answering,

"Of course my sister won't be there, she'll do as all women do, when I get the money hold out her hand!"

Harrison laughed confidently, not at what Moses said, but he was convinced the stupid thick Northerner didn't know his sister was dead. Then he answered confidently with his old arrogance.

"Okay you've got a deal. I'll see you there at seven, no tricks otherwise you die!"

Then Harrison put the phone down, Moses was again pleased with his handling of the conversation; once again he spoke aloud to himself,

"Now I've plenty of organising to do, I think I will end up with the Holy Grail with the half a million pounds; dancing on the grave of my sister's killers!

The first call Moses made was to an old girl friend, who was a dark haired beauty. As for her figure, the fall of her breasts was sight enough to rekindle a droopy wet lettuce on a Sunday morning.

A sweet feminine voice answered the phone, Moses' face broke into a warm smile; the voice washing over him reviving happy memories.

"How are you Jill its Moses?"

"Oh you didn't have to say I'd know that voice anywhere; how are you? Feeling lonely?"

"I'm always feeling lonely for you, only this time I want a favour, I want to hire your flat this evening for two hours; I'll pay you a hundred pounds."

"Well I will certainly accept your offer, A hundred pounds, you dear man; but I do hope there won't be any problems when you leave?

"I promise you my lady everything will be left as I found it."

The pretty young lady agreed, leaving Moses only one more call to make, it was to the smelly bar as the ugly bastard called it. A further deal was struck with two of the large coloured men, an evening's work for two hundred pounds. By eight o'clock all arrangements were made with the co-conspirators in position.

The road Moses had chosen was more of an alley, an enigmatic thoroughfare that was frozen in the past, Tudor style buildings overhung the narrow cobbled roadway; Moses carefully positioned himself at a window directly over the arranged confrontation.

The two hired assistants were told to stand at approximately a hundred yards along the alley, this careful arrangement Moses hoped; would bring the enemy directly below his window.

The evening light deserted the day, plunging the meeting place into darkness, enveloping his hired toughs; as they pushed themselves into the darkened corners of the alley.

While Moses sat at his window wearing all black—even a blacked out face, his designated position was a bedroom window, from there he hoped to gun down the entire group with his silenced weapon; Moses glanced at his watch urging the minutes to pass.

The window of the kitchen also over looked the target area, if Moses thought, he was unlucky enough to receive returning fire, and then he had an alternative position to fight from. This also may give the impression of two guns firing, outwardly giving a picture of formidable firepower.

After continually running through his mind the probable mishaps, that may occur during the forthcoming confrontation; then trying to pre-solve them, was beginning to give him a headache. So Moses decided to wait and see what might happen, in other words anticipate problems; but be ready to solve them!

CHAPTER 11
Retribution

Harrison sat at a desk in an office that was situated at the far end of a luxurious penthouse; that was his beautiful home in Mayfair. Turning a pencil in his hand from end to end, over and over and over; symbolic of the problem he was also turning over and over in his mind!

He really wanted the Grail; saying that he wanted the Grail was putting it mildly. In fact he yearned for it, lusted for it, most certainly willing to die for it, or kill for it. Desperation is a reckless driving force, which also breeds foolishness, Harrison knew this.

He hated dealing with the Northerner; he was more deadly than a rattlesnake. He'd already inspected the proposed meeting place for the exchange of money for the Grail, everything seemed straightforward.

How close he came to owning this priceless holy relic, only the two timing Moses ruined everything. Harrison stood up to look in the mirror, I swear to God and the Devil I will kill him so slowly he will be begging to die!

The bastard keeping me stuck inside this horrific looking shell, when I was so near to altering it, so near, so very near to improving it. Harrison could not control himself any more, he grabbed the mirror then threw it to the floor; in a mad frenzy jumped on it continually until he was exhausted; leaving under his feet, shards of scattered broken glass! Harrison slumped into an armchair, just for a moment he was drained of energy; then he thought about Friedman.

Tobias Friedman he must be the most disappointed, if it wasn't for me employing the killer Moses, the antique dealer would have put it straight into Friedman's hands. Harrison thought about the phone call he'd received from Friedman at the Mansion, the presence of Moses the killing machine causing Friedman to urge him to join forces with him against this predator. Moving in this company he thought is like swimming in the Florida swamps, trying to avoid being eaten by crocodiles.

Harrison stood up to gaze aimlessly out of the window across London's skyline, he knew it was a serious risk meeting the Paddy; bearing in mind Friedman did offer extra gunman to help him to exterminate the thug.

Can I trust this Friedman; I was never able to do so in the past—why should he change now. It was all matters of "If"—if—the Northerner succumbs to the attraction of the pile of money on offer then everything will be okay.

Supposing he knows his sister is dead, it could all go wrong and cost me my life. Although with a bit of luck he thought, I could end up owning the Grail, keeping it all to myself, also getting the opportunity to put the man called Moses down like the mad dog he is!

* * *

Moses sat in the dark with the window open wearing his overcoat with the collar turned up against the cold night air, waiting patiently. His two assistants had been given a square box similar to the one the enemy thinks they will be receiving; it was carried in a plastic Tesco bag.

Moses picked up the "walkie talkie" from the window cill to speak to his henchman,

"Can you hear me okay?"

The man on the other end answered in his deep rich Caribbean accent,

"Yeah man."

"Okay that's great, as soon as I think they've arrived I'll let you know. Don't forget to say what I told you. Stay tuned."

Moses sat back in his chair knowing his visitors would be late. Muttering aloud,

"It's all a matter of fucking mind games, sick load of bastards."

Moses checked every arrangement, he'd paid the two coloured boys in the street, his payment left in an envelope with the money in for the girl who owned the flat, and then suddenly his thoughts were interrupted by the entrance to the alley by three over-coated males. Moses quickly picked up the walkie-talkie garbling out a warning,

"The bastards are here!"

Moses pushed the chair he was sitting on as quietly as he could away from the window, and then knelt down in front of the opening, resting his elbows on the cill. Producing from his pocket his favourite weapon, a magnum with a silencer on the end, this tool will take no prisoners. He watched and waited for the newcomers to progress down the alley until they met the two coloured boys. Moses picked up the walkie talkie again whispering,

"Hello listen to me, move slowly out of the shadows let them see you, don't worry I have them covered."

Moses picked up his night binoculars to observe his henchman moving out slowly from the shadows. Moses spoke to them again over the machine,

"For fuck sake, speak to them call out to them!"

He heard the voice on the other end answer containing a note of irritation,

"Ok—ok man!"

Moses heard the sound from the street of the coloured boy calling out to them,

"Over here! Over here!"

The two coloured boys took the initiative advancing to the prearranged position under the window. There they stood patiently waiting for the few moments it would take for the visitors to join them. Moses couldn't wait; he slowly put down the night glasses then picked up his weapon.

As they moved forward he heard quite clearly the voice of the well-spoken sick bastard who led the attack on Teresa. Moses' finger gradually took up all the slack on the trigger, until quite clearly he heard the ultimate question,

"Where's the smart arse Moses?"

The coloured boy answered softly and submissively,

"He apologises for not being here but unfortunately a little problem cropped up with the police."

"It doesn't matter we'll get more sense out of you than a thick northerner!"

The words came up to Moses very clearly; the smile he wore would have put a crocodile to shame. The voice came up again,

"Is that the parcel?"

It was quickly answered again by a rich Caribbean accent.

"Yeah is that the fucking money man?"

It was at that moment Moses decided to end this meeting, three times Moses' weapon coughed, sounding like an old man's chest complaint! Harrison turned his head to see the two men by his side drop as he heard the spit of pistol fire, in that split second he also felt the hot poker enter his body causing him to fall by the side of his associates.

Laying there bleeding to death suddenly aware he was dying, in the closing seconds cursing his decision in not accepting Friedman's offer of assistance; now he was finished, all dreams will die, misplaced in the eternity of death, what a fool I've been. All these thoughts stumbling through his brain, as he felt the cold touch of steel to the back of his neck, bringing down the final curtain.

The third man, the well-spoken cold hearted old boy fell to the ground writhing on the floor with the pain from the bullet that blew his kneecap completely off, Moses closed his window dashing down the stairs slamming the door behind him. He slapped the big guy on the shoulder,

"Well done, it went like fucking clockwork, grab this old prat and throw him in the boot of my car. Forget about the other two; leave them for the pigs to clear away. But this one is mine." Moses first dropped to one knee to fire a bullet into the head's of Harrison and his thug as they lay in the shadow of death! Then he stood up to run, trying get ahead of his two assistants, carrying the groaning injured old man.

Moses stood with the old man in his arms as they opened the boot of his Jag then Moses dropped the groaning man in. The assassin reached into the side of the boot; groping around to find a roll of black tape proceeding to tape the old boy's eyes up, plus his mouth arms and legs.

In fact a pre-packed Sainsbury chicken had more free movement, ignoring the copious flow of blood amid the complaints of pain along with the whining words for mercy, as he slammed down the boot lid on the unfortunate passenger!

His two aides stood watching tacitly, they were more than a little shocked by the whole affair; for now they saw their hero in a totally different light. Not a political crusader, but a cruel cold killer, which made them feel even more apprehensive; forcing them to wonder if even they were going to survive this evil nights work. Moses looked at the two assistants, noticing the shocked expression on their faces, realising their insecurity triggered by his brutal actions to the wounded old man; prompting Moses to explain his cruelty.

"Don't worry about this old bastard, he's the man who led the attack on my sister; leaving her hanging from the ceiling naked, butchered like a cut of beef. Believe me I'll enjoy killing that man slowly; are you happy with your pay out? If you are I suggest you should make yourself scarce, the pigs are bound to join us shortly; thanks for your help."

Both of them just nodded vigorously to every word Moses said—who could blame them? Moses jumped into his Jag and drove away to meet Julie, joyously looking forward to the second part of his plan. As for the two coloured boys they watched Moses go in silence, both men thinking after what they had just witnessed, they were lucky to be paid and be alive.

* * *

Pilgrim sat waiting in a Chinese restaurant on the Edgware road with Chip, watching the rain bounce off the window. The man he had arranged to meet was an old acquaintance, a character he originally joined the agency with—called Peter Miles; he was a similar type build as him except for his looks. His face reflected a sort of battered look, his one sided nose with a scarred face from too many confrontations with the criminal element.

Among his colleagues it was well known if you were on a stake out that was going to end in a rough house, then Peter was the man to take with you; plus the fact he was a very good friend of Cunningham the chief of M I 6.

At last he entered the restaurant, glanced around then saw Pilgrim sitting with Chip; a smile breaking across his face as he strode over to join them.

"How are you old chap." He boomed as he stretched out his hand to Pilgrim then paused for a few seconds waiting for Pilgrim to introduce his friend which he did. Peter then sat down, a glass of wine was poured for him, amazingly in no time at all friendly banter broke across the table; as if the morning rain had washed away all the sombre tragedy over the last few years. Peter's face straightened into a serious mood as he asked,

"My old friend I'm pleased to see you but—also I am burning with curiosity to find out why after all these years you not only decide to call me but to add that it's urgent that you see me. Well here I am, tell me what you want; it will cure this twitch at the end of my nose."

Then he burst out laughing, moving into silence full of expectation. So Pilgrim, related in detail the whole story as he knew it; at first with a note of unnatural nervousness in his voice. Then after several minutes reverted to his old style of confidence with a touch of arrogance, Chip as Pilgrim was drawing to a close with his story ordered a bottle of wine then commenced to pour it; finishing pouring the wine as Pilgrim completed his tortuous account. Peter for several minutes sat staring at the pepper pot he was turning over again and again, then he looked up staring Pilgrim in the face with a long hard look as he spoke,

"I have to tell you Pilgrim, nobody who knew you could believe you were capable of killing a good friend like Trigger in cold blood, it was only the solidarity of the forensic evidence that eventually persuaded everybody of your guilt. Now of course with this shocking revelation, it's certainly a different situation. What do we do now? More to the point what are you doing now?"

At the asking of this very poignant question the two of them knew it would be impossible to answer, knowing most of the time they were continually breaking the law. So Chip replied in an almost instantaneous manner,

"Well believe it or not, we are for most of the time working for divorce lawyers." Peter rubbed his chin murmuring,

"Hmm I see, so you do have a little time to spare then. Can you trust me to take the evidence you have to sit and ponder on?"

This made Pilgrim squirm a little bit, the thought of losing this explosive evidence he had in his hand at the moment, would almost make him feel suicidal; but he knew if he couldn't trust this man then he should not have asked to meet him.

"I should not say this, I know I shouldn't but you do realise these two men have ruined my life, murdered my good friend Trigger; also without doubt the stress of it indirectly responsible for the cancerous related death of my wife. So it needs no emphasising on my part, to tell you to look after these documents with your life, I'm hoping its pay back time; God only knows I have waited long enough!"

Peter nodded with a look of grim seriousness on his battered features,

"Of course Pilgrim, please have no fear I'm *on your side*; leave it all with me for a few days, by then I'm sure I'll have it all sown up." His clear well spoken words coupled with his natural overt attitude convinced Pilgrim, to trust Peter as he always had done in the past, so Pilgrim handed over the valuable package. Pilgrim's trusted warrior friend stood up then shook hands with our adventurers, leaving the restaurant, carrying under his arm all the hopes and fears in a parcel of retribution; aimed at the people who designed this awful intricate web of deceit!

CHAPTER 12
The Way Young Women Are!

J ulie looked in the mirror, her face was quite flushed, she put her hands to her face, feeling the burning that had overcome her, and she was unusually very excited at how events had moved so fast. Encouraging her to speak aloud to herself in a Hamlet like manner,

"I will definitely buy myself something really smart; I certainly won't let my brother down. I just wish I could find his mobile number, I wonder if it is in that old blue short coat the one I haven't worn for some time."

Julie moved to her wardrobe pushing her way through the clothes, commenting on different outfits she either liked or hated.

Suddenly finding the suit she was looking for, pulling it from the rack to throw it on the bed. Julie then searched every pocket carefully, until she was rewarded for her efforts. Pulling the odd scrap of paper from the small hip pocket, momentarily studying the number scrawled on the paper, and then released a sigh of significant satisfaction; as she moved eagerly to the bedside table to use her phone.

"Mister Mystery will have a shock when he hears how I've tracked him down so easily!"

Julie sat there eagerly listening to her phone ringing her brother's mobile,

"Oh come on pick it up you great nana."

The voice on the other end informed Julie the phone was unattended—but she could leave a message after the tone, so she instead used her long slender fingers to send a text; informing Chip of her date with his good friend Moses! Hmm—she thought wait till he finds that little message on his phone!!

* * *

Pilgrim closed the door then switched on the light; he had agreed to set up the surveillance duties on these other gangsters; while Chip ran the errands for the food. Pilgrim took off his jacket, turned to throw it towards the chair by the window, as he threw it he suddenly saw the stranger sitting in the armchair.

The stranger caught the jacket dropping it down by the side of him exuding great arrogance, Pilgrim recognised the individual instantly, it was one of the characters who framed him for the killing of his colleague; the sight of him caused Pilgrim to speak this character's name aloud.

"Jim Donohugh!" Donohugh's face broke into a sneering smile, while Pilgrim for a second froze; their eyes locked into a dog like stare of aggressive masculinity.

Pilgrim broke the silence first, with a sound that could have been mistaken for more of a snarl,

"What does a fucking rat like you want?"

"Why are you talking to me in that tone of voice Pilgrim? After all it wasn't me that killed your friend Trigger."

Pilgrim answered in a soft voice full of hatred,

"I don't suppose it was—you most likely left that dirty little job to your friend Ronnie Gomaz."

The man in the chair sat there for a while shaking his head before he spoke,

"Is it my fault you listen to a man that tells you fairy tales, I know and you know you were caught bang to rights for the killing of John Tregear, you served your time so now you have got to get on with your life; that is if you want a life to get on with, the choice is yours!"

"Tell me, did I sense a threat attached to those few words?

The crooked M I 6 agent smiled confidently as he answered,

"You are intelligent enough to realise the people you are playing with are very powerful, they will of course react ruthlessly once again, as they did before to anyone subscribing to the investigation of the man called slippery Sam, I am not here to warn you off; I'm here to advise you against doing anything, that could jeopardise your well being!"

Pilgrim could not control himself any longer, he moved so fast across the room. The mendacious character sitting in the chair, whose only purpose to be there was to threaten a great lump like Pilgrim! He never got the chance to use the gun in his pocket, Pilgrim had this thick skinned liar by his throat lifting him up from the chair spluttering, wriggling and choking, like a sprat caught on the end of a fishing line.

Pilgrim was now loaded up and ready to kill as if he was an automatic firearm, this uninvited guest had just been tinkering with the trigger; now he didn't like the result. Pilgrim head butted him twice, blood spewed forth from his nostrils then Pilgrim pulled back his size fifteen fist to pound his head to a pulp just as Chip entered the room. Chip recognised instantly the killing mode of frenzy Pilgrim was switched into, so he very quickly called for Pilgrim to stop.

"Pilgrim for fuck sake! "

Chip rushed across the room to stop Pilgrim from damaging this epigone any further; with blood splashed across his face that also spilt down his shirt. The man who came into the room to threaten Pilgrim was now hanging in rags fearing for his life, falling back into the chair like a blooded sack of potatoes; when let go by the powerful hands of Pilgrim, prompted by Chip. Chip stood in front of the injured individual knowing full well Pilgrim was going to kill him,

"Calm your self down Pilgrim for fucks sake! You want this bastard in front of a jury not a coroner—that would be too easy! Pilgrim moved his head around the body of Chip to speak in a way that told this treacherous M I 6 man he was still in great danger,

"You can think your self lucky he stopped me!"

The man sunk deeper into the chair as his hand struggled to pull his gun from his pocket, but Chip's revolver suddenly appeared in his hand so fast a western gunfighter would have been proud of the action, he then mendaciously pushed his weapon into the man's temple. Chip spoke slowly moving his mouth to speak clearly,

"Take the gun from your pocket then throw it on the floor!" The blood soaked vulpine character did exactly as he was told, then sat in the chair unmoving ignoring the dripping blood from his badly bruised nose attempting to dye his shirt—and succeeding. Pilgrim was still very fired up desperately wanting to finish off the work he had started, only the palm of Chip's hand held lightly on his chest kept him at bay, while Pilgrim struggled to find the words to describe the situation,

"Chip I could not believe my eyes when this bastard was sitting in the chair when I entered the room, he then started to bait me as if I was some sort of caged animal."

As Pilgrim finished speaking there was a light tap on the door, the two men stood motionless for several seconds, suddenly the whole world seem to be full of there enemies all wanting them dead. Chip made motions with his hand for Pilgrim to answer the door, as Pilgrim opened the door Chip moved across the room to an angle where he covered the door and the bloodied fox in the chair.

They were surprised to see it was Peter Miles; he pushed his way into the room, to stand staring at Donohugh in the chair.

"What did you intend doing with this creature? Killing him?" Pilgrim answered the question in a quiet sardonic voice,

"I must admit that was nearly on the agenda, but as Chip pointed out, we would prefer to see him in front of a Jury at the Old Bailey!"

Peter Miles strode across the room, as he did so gave the arrested conspirator a curt order to stand, when he did Peter spun him around as if he was a package of nonentity, then deftly applied a set of handcuffs on his wrists, then he turned to address his two good friends,

"I'm sorry to intrude like this, on receiving from you the documents containing such damning evidence against this man along with his fellow operator; the decision was taken to act as if this whole affair was an emergency. Also you were both followed in case you were needed, we know from the past how you Pilgrim can vanish into the underworld.

This man is now mine—also you will be glad to hear, he is being arrested for the killing of your colleague Tregear; along with several other charges of conspiracy and treason!"

Pilgrim could not believe his ears,

"All this is happening so quickly isn't it? To me only moments ago I took this as being a Sisyphean task, this is really unbelievable!"

Peter's face adopted a mask of gravity as he answered,

"Pilgrim I didn't hesitate, you and I realised it was a desperate situation so I went straight to the top with the information you gave me to discuss it with our top man Cunningham; who as you know still holds you in very high regard.

I know you spent a lot of time in jail for this, but Cunningham's head is now on the line, this situation is a great big embarrassment for the whole department, appreciating of course your terribly tortuous experience Pilgrim.

Then this awful person Slippery Sam's place was raided, ultimately revealing the whole story which I might add included many others also, it's only a matter of time before you will be notified of your innocence. There is in additional warrant issued for the arrest of Alfred Etherington along with the junior minister Wenham, you are going to be famous when this news hits the streets! Thank the good Lord you didn't kill this scum, otherwise you could have been the one I was arresting; now that would have been a tragedy!" Peter turned to go and take the handcuffed man with him, but was stopped by Pilgrim,

"Please before you go—you must tell me Peter, how close were we—Trigger and I in catching these pair of high class villains? I am of course referring to the two ministers."

Peter smiled at Pilgrim knowing that during those years in prison he must have been eating his brain out not knowing whether or not it really was these two ministers who were directly responsible for his false imprisonment.

"Pilgrim you were so close they must have been filling their pants, to adopt the killing policy they did, and then scheme to have you put away for it, this time however they really are going to pay the price. You know that when the department finds people who are responsible for damaging their officers, there's the Devil to pay and the Devil will be paid for this one in full; anyway Pilgrim—I'll be in touch—don't forget you owe me a large Whiskey old chap!"

Peter then disappeared through the door, bundling the moaning blood stained figure before him. Leaving Pilgrim with Chip to stand and stare at each other, stunned. Chip smiled at Pilgrim adding,

"I really don't know what to say to you, but congratulations."

Pilgrim sort of half nodded in a typical English stoical way then turned to sit down by the window, he answered with silence; in spite of his half American breeding! Chip could feel the pain and hatred bubbling forth from Pilgrim, but there was nothing he could do or say to mend the wounds or dispel the scars; so he added very quickly

"I'll go and get the food, I'm bloody starving."

Pilgrim walked across the room then switched off the light, drawing the curtains to enable him to resume his watch. While his eyes carried out his orders, there was no way he could stop his mind from retracing the past, Pilgrim's thoughts raced back into the past years of his married life like everyone—there were some turbulent times.

The surprising reflections of trying to revive the memories of the good times, to Pilgrim were similar to rescuing the erotic sculpture of the kiss; buried in a muddy hole. Then blasting away the dirt and the grime revealing the depth of love and romance in the action of the kiss, symbolic of all the good years, wrapped in the muddy problems in the past of sporadic good and bad years!

His thoughts traversed away from those times right through to the first day he was finally imprisoned to face the onset of lonely nights, when the reality of the situation pounced upon him like a ravenous tiger tearing at his mind and soul. While his pent up aggression turned into hate against the whole world to even question the good Lord himself, knowing he was innocent turned his stomach;

not understanding why this terrible miscarriage of justice had trapped him in prison or even happened at all.

Even on his parole when his wife didn't want him initially, unbelievably she needed time to accept he was a paroled prisoner guilty of manslaughter; he never knew to this day how he survived all that with a smile on his face. Remembering clearly how he shut Julie out of his world, terrified of weaving further complications into his life, but at the same time the offer of no strings attached with the genuine compassion she gave, appreciating his tenuous unhappy position in life.

Pilgrim knew deep down although almost frightened to admit to himself, it was only Julie's concern with her pure sympathetic caring attitude massaging away the hurt that stopped him from taking his own life; that's how desperate he was. As for Julie most of the time he even felt more guilty over her, her love and concern for him always reminded him of a beleaguered rose in a shaded forest reaching out trying to find just a little sunlight in her life by her loving association with him; that at the time he couldn't repay!

The sad part was the guilt he carried, all the time knowing he had not committed any crime, but sadly aware that there was no point in trying to tell anybody, because it would only bring a wry smile to the face of cynical listeners! Not knowing, that all the time the men who did this to him, were working beside him within the legal framework of M I 6.

Those two politicians who were responsible for the absolute architecture of the framework in every sense of the word, created such immense treachery that destroyed my world; the fact that they are about to be punished fills me with extreme satisfaction! My life now feels as if it is straightening out, now that would be a new experience.

The trouble is all the time there is this nagging feeling knawing at me, how is the wheelchair man at the mansion connected with this side of my life—for surely he is; to make the statement so definitely defining my innocence! Pilgrim turned his eyes away from the window to witness Chip enter with the fish and chips, the smell made him feel even hungrier.

Then Pilgrim dropped his eyes to the floor noticing Chip's cell phone half hidden under the settee. He bent to pick it up handing it to Chip as he spoke; still really in a state of shock;

"I really find it hard to believe this nightmare is over!"

Chip took the cell phone from Pilgrim, automatically glancing at the dial to see if there were any calls, noticing there was a message framed in the window of the machine, he then flicked through the controls to check any messages; expecting one to be from Tobias.

When he read the text message from Julie realising what she was saying he broke into a cold sweat. They both sat on the bed while Chip read out aloud the message for Pilgrim to hear, Pilgrim's face also drained white.

"Chip do we know how long that message has been on your cell phone?" Chip shrugged his shoulders rubbing his face with his hands expelling a loud sigh as he spoke with emphasis on each word.

"Honestly I haven't got a clue; I'd even forgotten I had the phone. You know what women are like; they secrete phone numbers away like bloody squirrels! The point is there's only one thing we can do now—go and get her, that is if she's still alive!"

"Chip we have to do this but you and I know it may well cost both our lives, but we have no choice. Come on let's go, we'll phone her on the way!" The fish and chips were left to go cold and unwanted.

CHAPTER 13
The Search Begins

The thugs entering the room could see Toby wasn't a happy bunny; in fact he was seething with rage, moulding his face into a heavy scowl as black as thunder. They stood silently waiting for the cauldron to boil over, and it did.

"Do I pay you clowns all this money for such incompetence, do you know Harry is dead; killed in my own house while the perpetrator walked free!

In fact Harry wasn't found until two hours after the killing, tell me in confidence are you absolute idiots, or are you all just mentally retarded?" Tobias paused for moment to survey the sorry looking bunch he'd surrounded himself with. They said nothing, standing in silence for they too were stunned by the killing of an old friend; who was directly responsible for their personal recruitment, to such a cushy little highly paid job.

After running his eyes around this bunch of what he regarded as reticent fools, Tobias lowered his voice in a very menacing tone.

"Do you think you can offer an explanation?"

Again Tobias paused, waiting for one of the gang of thugs to offer some sort of deceitfully contrived excuse, but nothing was forthcoming.

"Well do you think it possible for one of you to string a line of adjectives together explaining the chain of events prior to the killing of Harry?"

One of the thugs cleared his throat hesitating for a second, then garbled out his view of what happened, his nick name totally reflecting his mentality.

"Keyboard" because he was only capable of doing things if the right buttons were pushed in a very clear and definite manner, but unable to act very successfully on his own independent thinking; but he was a very big man and capable of extreme violence.

Crooked employers were happy to use Keyboard because of exactly that, he gave complete loyalty to whosoever paid his wages, doing what ever he was asked to do, legal, or illegal, or just plain and simple beating some unfortunate to a pulp. So this day he was unused to catching the rough edge of anyone's tongue, desperate to offer the reason why none of them knew Harry was dead; in his own inimitable London's East End accent!

"It's like this boss—we offered to go wiv im cos we knew 'e was a tricky customer, but 'arry insisted he was alright on his own, in fact he told us to go to bed and not to worry."

Here the brainless thug shrugged his shoulders like a wayward six-year-old,

"You know what 'arry was like guv, alright it was wrong, we never fought for a minute 'arry ed get it did we, we're as choked as you are. We just want to go and get this geezer."

Keyboard looked down at his feet shuffling the floor showing a certain amount of embarrassment, then muttered the words.

"Only we don't know where to go and get im, we fought you'd tell us Guv." The wheelchair man sat looking at Keyboard in wonderment, and then shook his head not knowing whether to laugh or cry before speaking in a low voice again.

"I suppose you are not aware that this man had the complete run of the house while you slept on like babies, he was also given the opportunity to rifle through all my precious records. Presenting him on a plate the addresses of all his enemies, I think we will find him pursuing Chip's sister. He will use her to lay a trap for Chip and Pilgrim, I only hope you manage to get there in time otherwise you might well find the two of them turning their attentions to a bunch of losers like you lot.

If our friend Mister Moses isn't there when you arrive, please be patient wait out of sight for him to appear; when he does—follow him—but not before notifying Pilgrim and Chip! "

Ernie decided it was his turn to ask a question, he was much brighter than Key board, he being part thug part hoist man as they say in the criminal world for anybody who is a bank robber. Unfortunately for Ernie the long arm of the law became too conversant with his handy work, so he ended up doing what he considered a soft job working for somebody else, only this time he thought to ask the question they all wanted to know.

"Er if you don't mind me asking how did you come to that conclusion?"

Tobias drew in a deep breath before he answered,

"I'm tempted to say just trust me, but I'll tell you. The file on Chip's sister was found on the floor, which represents too much of a coincidence. So please, you will find all the instructions you will need on the kitchen table. Bring me back this damn Northerner dead or alive; one important point gentlemen do try to do it in a subtle manner, which will evade the attentions of our friends the blue suited gentlemen."

The three villains left the room with resolute faces, angry but dedicated to redeem themselves from this pit of humiliation. Keyboard with the rest of the hired muscle sped away from their headquarters, as Tobias watched from a floor to ceiling landing window, their departure down the long drive. He turned to look up and smile at the ageing secretary standing by the side of him, a man of about sixty, slightly built who at a glance anybody could see he was an accountant; a man who carried that slight ambience of Scrooge!

"I hate to say this Ronald, but I think the man they call Moses is too smart for all four of those thugs that have just left."

The secretary's face never moved a muscle as he answered in a very well educated manner, showing a good command with clear upper class pronunciation of the English language.

"Well those men you refer to have quite good credentials to do the job you've asked them to do but, as you know from my CV I have served time in many government institutions for either fraud or conspiring to commit fraudulent conversion; but of course not anything violent. I do personally know of these men and their violent ways for I have acted as an accountant on behalf of most of them, whether or not they can cope with the professional trained personnel of the Patriotic British Party of course remains to be seen sir."

"Well said Ron—well said, I could not have put it better myself, it makes me feel it was worth the trouble to drag you up here to take the place of Harry."

"If you don't mind me asking sir, bearing in mind that I'm the new boy here, why do you want this Northerner so badly, is he so important?"

This forthright question brought a scowl to the face of the man in the wheel chair as he answered,

"Ronald I have noted you have asked rather a leading question, one actually under normal circumstances I would ignore. The situation is so ironic that I don't mind sharing it with you, for a long time now I been aware of a traitor in the camp.

Knowing this, gave me an opportunity to feed this character with false information; which fitted in very well with my plans. Always hoping to find out the whereabouts and name of the enemy that continually outfoxed me, the nearest to finding the answer to that problem was to capture the Northerner, then make him divulge that secret.

Harry's insistence to go and tend to the prisoner himself was born of his intention to release the Paddy; this of course would embrace asking the prisoner to make it look as if it was a real breakout. Unfortunately our captive didn't know my butler was on his side, unbelievable isn't it."

The secretary blinked a few times then thought for a moment, then asked yet another question,

"If you knew Harry was a traitor—why did you let him deal with the hostage?"

"It's quite easy really; I never wanted to let Harry know I was onto him, but never thought for one moment, the other hirelings would let my butler handle the hostage on his own. Bearing in mind he was responsible for them being employed in the first place, I thought they would automatically be too concerned for Harry's safety to let him handle such a dangerous character alone; so that's how and why the sequence of events occurred, easy wasn't it."

"Excuse me Sir, I might be a little new for this but if Harry was a traitor and the other thugs were thankful to him for their employment, how do you know they all weren't traitors?"

The wheelchair man burst out laughing then talked through the laughter,

"I don't, or should I say I didn't—but I'm certain that if they were in the pay of the enemy, they most certainly would have accompanied Harry to see the Paddy, I'm almost sure they are not in the pay of the enemy; but on the other hand they might be."

Tobias looked at his watch,

"In about fifteen minutes time a car will arrive manned by people who have been in my employ for many years, tried and trusted. Come we need to move quickly, by the time we reach the ground floor the car will arrive."

"Before we leave sir one more question, what about this Chip and Pilgrim what will happen to them?"

"Oh I've no need to worry about them anymore, they will be dead within twenty four hours, that is if the three thugs turn out to be traitors as well, if they stay true to me, Chip and Pilgrim might, and I mean might, just survive."

Tobias motioned irritably with his hand as he spoke the next few words.

"Come on—come on we have to move quickly now!"

The secretary still wore a confused look on his face insisting on pursuing the point, which confused him to the end.

"Excuse me sir, there are many facets of these happenings that still confuse me, namely why are you doing this, so far throughout the conversation you never gave a reason for any of these escapades?" Tobias's face twisted up into a moronic rage, speaking through his clenched teeth he spoke quietly with control.

"Please will you step around in front of me before I can answer your question?

The dapper little secretary stepped around in front of the wheelchair inhabitant, eager to hear the information about certain facets that triggered his curiosity, eager to hear answers. The wheel chair man looked up at the face of the questioner trying hard not to show his rage, speaking again in a very quiet voice.

"Please bend down a little nearer to me; I want to make sure you hear every word I say."

The bespectacled naive weasel of a man bent down nearer to the hands of his employer, never knowing or realising the omens of danger flashing across Tobias's face as he did so. The hands of Tobias moved in an instant to clasp the throat of the small non violent unwary listener, choking him to the edge of death as he spoke in a quiet rasping threatening tone!

"I never brought you here to act as my inquisitor, do you think you are addressing some little fart of a tax officer. If you wish to live to an old age never never ask any questions, just do as you are told!"

Tobias let go of the choking man throwing him to the floor, then sat watching him slowly recover from the almost strangled state, coughing and choking, struggling to scramble to his feet. When the pathetic little character had almost recovered, then finally straightening the frames of his glasses to replace them on his nose; a nose that was most certainly not going to be poked into his employers business again? He stood trembling, blinking with fear; not knowing whether or not he was going to live or die.

For only in prison had he experienced such spiteful aggression at the hands of a known violent maniac, but was fortunate to be saved by the men whose businesses he helped to run. The little man stood there for a few minutes studied by his assailant, until the silence was broken by an order from his employer.

"Come on get me downstairs, we've wasted too much time already!

The little man moved in a significantly subdued manner, moving without question to his employer's demands!

CHAPTER 14
A Night to Remember

The tall slim blonde Northerner, arrived outside Julie's flat ten minutes early, the brand new silver Jaguar sports car he was driving nosed its sleek shiny body into the kerb adjacent to Julie's flat; turning a few heads in admiration on its way into the parking space. Moses checked once again in the rear view mirror, to inspect his make up talents—covering his facial bruising, he was quite satisfied, that the few marks which were on view he'd be able to explain away without any problems.

Moses picked up his mobile phone to dial Julie's number, drumming his knee with the fingers of his left hand impatiently; while waiting for her to answer. He was pertinently aware that the occupants of the mansion would soon be after him that is if they weren't around right now. The importance of this Julie answering this call plus his ability to convince her to completely trust him; was paramount to the completion of his hell bent Satan's mission!

At last the pretty jingle of her very feminine voice answered, so Moses informed her enthusiastically he was waiting for her to join him in a dash to paradise. Julie laughed, telling him she would be right down, replaced the receiver—took another glance in the mirror using her hand to flick her hair just once more as a women does; picking up her coat at the same time as the phone rang again, of course it was her brother Chip!

Her hand hovered over the top of the handset just for a second listening to it's demanding bell but then—decided against answering it, her preference fuelled by a woman's curiosity to what was waiting for her downstairs, inciting the pretty girl to run off down the steps as if her feet were attached to wings; with only the thought of this mysterious paramour foremost in her mind.

Until suddenly in that flashing thought, remembered her text message to Chip; wondering if that call was from her beloved brother acknowledging her message. In those precious passing seconds decided against that probability, then proceeded to pursue her personal plans, so parcelled within that moment the format of destiny was formed. Slamming the door to the flat behind her as she rushed through it, unknowingly, not realising that the final action of the closing door symbolically reflected the end of her association to that former life as she once knew it!

* * *

Pilgrim drove through the traffic as quickly as was humanly possible, hoping no traffic police were around. They both sat in silence for most of the journey, feeling quite numb; the thought of Julie in the company of the assassin made both men feel deeply concerned. In troubled times such as this Pilgrim always thought about his parents, who proved to be such stalwart supporters throughout the troubled times of his imprisonment, who were also a major crutch on his release.

Especially when his wife found it difficult to accept his conviction, or believe his story of innocence; she was of course like her parents, deeply influenced with the sombre infections of a middle class back ground; convinced that the arm of the law is never wrong! While he also found it hard to accept her initial repugnance of him as a man; whom he thought she would have accepted and loved him through this crisis in his life!

He remembered quite clearly how he almost ran back to America, to escape this vilification from his wife's family; inflaming his yearning for the beautiful Julie, knowing this association could jeopardise the mental and physical security of his children.

Pilgrim wondered what his father would have thought of this threat to Julie, not a lot I don't think, one thing is for sure if ever I manage to survive this latest round of events, I will look forward to telling him of the public announcement of my absolution! Through all these thoughts, the same question kept running through his mind.

How did this evil creature from the swamps of low life, manage to capture beautiful Julie? Did this evil hit man shoot his way out of the Victorian Mansion? Or was he released to intimidate Chip and me? None of it seemed to make any sense; perhaps the only one who could enlighten them would be the wheelchair man himself—Tobias!

Pilgrim broke away from the mental merry go round of unanswerable questions to curse the traffic; he certainly was getting pissed off with the heavily blocked roads with home going people and cars. One thing is for certain if the Paddy has hurt Julie in any way I'll empty the whole magazine into the bastard, this immature mental threat brought solace to his troubled mind; even if it did bring an adolescent attitude to the situation

"We've changed you know Chip, since we started this job; I suppose the change was inevitable."

Chip never answered right away but sat thinking for awhile about Pilgrim's conclusions, he then answered adding his small analogy to Pilgrim's philosophies.

"Well you know what they say about the police force, because of the every day filth they mix with, they end up the same. With all this killing and violence how could we remain unaffected? I can only hope and pray we manage to save my Julie from the same fate as the poor lady hanging from the light, I wonder if he sees Julie in the same way as we saw his sister?" That is of course—in a loving caring way?

Pilgrim shook his head as he answered,

"I really don't know how we can know the state of such twisted minds, his evil activities obviously now amounts to revenge, I suppose he took a beating from the thugs at the mansion.

So now he blames us for all his troubles, a package which not only embraces his being captured then taken back to the mansion; but also the death of his sister. His planned hit most likely consists of the old man, then us or us then the old man. What more can I say!"

Chip nodded in agreement as he answered,

"Every thing you say makes sense; I have a terrible feeling that by the time we get to her flat she will be gone."

"Chip if she's gone by the time we get there how are we going to get into her flat?"

"That's not too much of a problem. As long as the next door neighbour's in, strangely enough although the two front doors are in totally different places, Julie's being in between the shop fronts and the neighbours at the back of the block; the flats are identical. From the lounge they have similar balconies; you can climb from one flat to the other, without a problem. So if Julie is out let's hope the neighbours are in."

Pilgrim nodded then remained quiet for a time, so did Chip. Their nerves screwed up like coiled springs, urging a clear path through the evening traffic, while so many questions remained unanswered appertaining to this oddesy they were caught up in; motivating Pilgrim to pose more questions to Chip!

"You know I'm still amazed that we really don't know the final actual reason for this whole escapade, the thought of trying to track down the Holy Grail seems a bit far fetched. But after seeing the temple in the mansion, then also hearing a few comments from our employer; makes me think that's what we're after!"

Chip turned to look at Pilgrim as he spoke,

"What did you mean when you said about the comments from our employer?"

"Well think about it, do you remember how he emphasised the time when he would be walking again, in a funny way it was as if he was referring to the special powers of the Grail; I get a weird feeling he's all mixed up with the black art; I could be talking complete rubbish it's just that it sort of points that way to me." Chip laughed,

"Perhaps you're right, well if we're working for the bad guys who are the good guys? Possibly we will meet them shortly."

Chip and Pilgrim banged on the door of Julie's next door neighbour, then stood waiting for an answer.

The sound of movement came from inside; the front door was opened by a short fat little man smartly dressed in a suit with a friendly jovial face. Pilgrim stood silent while Chip spoke to the man,

"Hello Chip how are you?"

The little man's face split into a grin when he saw Chip and was quick to shake hands with him, asking at the same time,

"What can I do for you Chip? Goodness it's a long time since I've seen you!"

Chip smiled back answering,

"Well you know how it goes with work, it's all or nothing. I've been so very busy that I' thought I'd call in to see my sister, unfortunately I forgot my key and she's out, so I wondered if it would be possible to jump over your balcony; I really would like to go in and wait for her to return."

The short fat little man was only too pleased to accommodate Chip and Pilgrim, so in no time at all they were sitting in Julie's lounge drinking tea—hoping and praying for her safe return.

* * *

The restaurant Moses and Julie were sitting in was a popular grazing spot in London for all the celebrities, fortunately for Moses he knew the millionaire owner of the restaurant, for he was from the same home town, Rochdale. Julie was duly impressed; and rather taken back by the good looks accompanied by the softly spoken accent used by the polished ladies man, sitting in front of her.

The meal was as expected—superb, better still Moses knew the girl sitting in front of him was impressed, and so because of the surroundings was becoming very malleable. The plan he'd prepared to kill the two cocky bastards who captured him, who were the cause of the vicious beatings he'd taken was beginning to work very well. Sitting in the corner of the same restaurant was a very thick set flat nosed character in the company of another man who also looked like an escapee from a gangster movie.

Tall very dark, broad yet expensively dressed, obviously not a brain surgeon but definitely one who works with his hands. The pair was duly noticed by Moses, causing his brain to work overtime for he never reckoned on any extra company at this stage.

The handsome young couple finished eating, Julie was sitting on cloud seven thinking what a wonderful man this was sitting in front of her, ready to fall into his arms at the least invitation, after all her own brother asked him to call her, what better recommendation than that. Moses leaned across the table speaking in a low gentle voice.

"Do you fancy coming over to my place for a cup of coffee Julie?" Julie's heart was pumping when she heard the words, in as much as she thought this man was a wonderful guy; she did not want to seem too eager. Of course she wanted to go, it seemed an age since she was with such an attractive companion; leaving Julie hoping this was one relationship that would get off to a good start.

Julie was sick of meeting the wrong guys, either they were good guys and married or single and bad guys. Now this one was better than all her hopes, she was getting sick of falling for men like Pilgrim; whom she loved very much but who never paid her any attention. Oh yes she knew in her heart she was wasting her time carrying a torch for the likes of him, he would never leave his wife, perhaps in this man she had at last found the right one.

At the same time she was quick to make a lame excuse, that work the next day was something that stood in the way of a late night. A look of exaggerated disappointment suddenly masked Moses' face with the worded plea,

"Come on baby don't spoil the evening, I've arranged something nice for you!"

Julie hesitated genuinely concerned that every thing was getting out of control; maybe she was being manipulated into something she would regret. Her brother Chip no doubt would say she was being a prude, but never the less Julie very quickly decided that she was not going to go; Chip can call me what he likes, but that is the end of it. She also put on the look of a woman that was really sorry; reaching out to touch the blonde assassin's hand as she spoke, creating a sense of sincerity!

"Look I'm really sorry but I have a very busy day tomorrow, a late night is not acceptable. Please forgive me; another night would be very nice."

The blonde killer leaned back in his chair speaking through a half yawn,

"Oh that's fine I understand, another time will be fine; I'll just have to keep that little something for you in a special place until the next time. The evening has been wonderful, as for you well, your brother might know you as a sister but not as a pretty attractive woman; it's a pleasure being in your company."

The words made Julie blush a little, such flattery was unashamedly delightful to her. Moses paid the bill; then the couple made their way out of the restaurant to the Jaguar.

Key board sat in the eating house, carefully noting the couple leaving in a manner that was as unassuming as possible, he couldn't help but notice how angelic the man accompanying Julie was; reminding him of a former friend who was no longer around because he was such a violent head case.

In as much as he used to fool people with his angelic looks until he became well known, and then of course fellow thugs were aware of his dangerous appetite for violence. Keyboard turned to his companion,

"You can see the guys a head case and no doubt very tricky, I hope Bert is still in the street and not fallen sleep?"

Harry—his friend, smiled as he answered,

"No danger of that he's the best wheel man in the business."

Key board nodded as he spoke,

"I think we ought to sit here until Bert gives us a bell to tell us when the Paddy has reached his destination don't you?"

Moses got into the car watching Julie put her pretty legs in, and then duly sat in the front seat next to her. Moses reached behind Julie's seat feeling in the dark for a looped rope.

"Julie please shut your eyes, please don't open them until I tell you; I have something for you."

A big grin split across her face so she shut her eyes instantly wondering what on earth this lovely person beside her had in his hand for her!

Moses leant forward kissing Julie gently on her mouth as he did she could hear the rustling behind her then something being slipped over her head very carefully, next she could swear was the sound of sticky tape being pulled. All sorts of beautiful thoughts ran through her mind, it was a parcel, that's why the sound of tape, of course it was a parcel being undone.

Then suddenly it was being stuck across her mouth and the something that was once a present was being pulled over her head; it was pulled so tight she couldn't move her arms or scream out. She opened her eyes to see the lovely smiling blonde northerner, sitting beside her as calm as a vicar at a wedding. Julie's brain was racing trying to find an explanation for this outrageous behaviour but couldn't find any.

Moses stroked her hair very gently as he spoke, unfortunately she could not help noticing the absolute jubilance in his voice.

"I'm very sorry to do this to you but I have no choice, I have to use you to get your brother and his accomplice. You see they were responsible for putting me into a very tricky situation, well it's all about payback time my dear Julie!"

Julie couldn't believe her ears, what a mistake she'd made; she knew in the past, the golden rule was she never went out with or associated with anybody who was supposedly a friend of Chip's; until she'd spoken in person to Chip!

Julie sat in wide eyed terror, every muscle in her body tensed up not knowing what was going to happen next, worse still cursing herself for being so damn stupid. The man called Moses started the car then drove away, Julie could hear him laughing saying aloud,

"I'll get the bastards now I have the bate!"

CHAPTER 15
The Games People Play!

Pilgrim eyes darted around the room, he thought and wondered deeply about how they had landed in this predicament and not for one minute did either of them think they'd entangle Julie in this arbitrary game of whose turn it is to die? Then I suppose the way my life has unfolded of late, death has had a habit of following my footsteps.

What about my children? I haven't even had time to think about them, or even talk to them. Thank goodness they are away in boarding school, tucked up and safe from all these gutter rats. Julie—my lovely Julie! What an awful worry all this has turned out to be.

It was bad enough when we realised this was a game of death, as for us men—well the way I feel at the moment if I snuffed it who would really worry about it! My parents would take care of the children, and there's no one else to care. Sitting here like this is a nightmare, that angel faced bastard is so full of guile.

It's about one year ago, when we found out my wife was dying of cancer, now it's all over; time can be such a good friend but also a tiresome enemy— Pilgrim thoughts were interrupted by the ringing of the telephone.

Suddenly both men stiffened, rushing to the phone, which was the other side of the room on the sideboard; Chip got there first—carefully lifting the receiver placing it against his ear; the fear of what he might hear already showing on his face,

"Hello, this is Julie's brother talking."

The voice on the other end of the phone cleared his throat before he spoke; the voice was not immediately recognisable.

"Hello Chip is that you, you don't really know me but I know you, I work for Toby at the mansion, we were ordered to go and find the assassin; we arrived at your sister's flat just as he was driving away with your sister in the car. Anyway, we followed him to a restaurant in the West End, when they finished their meal, the Paddy left with her; one of our wheel men followed them to a crematorium in North London.

Now we are here watching the place, it's a building that's surrounded by woods with one road in, the large iron gates were left open; of course our target drove in as if he knew the place well. We were hoping you would come to join us here, perhaps we can nail the bastard!" Chip's brain was racing, asking himself all sorts of questions. I think I know the voice speaking but don't really know for sure if this man is really genuine or on our side, if he is—well and good but—but—. Chip decide to go along with this person on the other end of the phone, so he drew a deep breath winking at Pilgrim; then proceeded to make the arrangements to meet him.

"Okay, tell me where this place is, and we'll get their ASAP." The gruff East End accented voice explained to Chip exactly where the crematorium was, but before the guy could ring off Chip asked him one more question.

"Before you go please tell me how this wanker got away?" The guy on the other end paused for a moment before resuming in a gruff East London accent,

"Well you remember the fella who was Toby's butler, he made the mistake of releasing one of the Paddy's hands, he must have had a knife up his sleeve and done poor old 'arry in the froat wiv it. It was simple as that, 'arry insisted in going up to feed him 'isself. Any way we'll lookout for ya."

Chip was left listening to the dialling tone of the phone—standing there letting all this flood of information sink into his brain, only then did he replace the receiver turning to speak to Pilgrim. As he did the phone rang again, Chip looked at Pilgrim gesturing for him to get it this time. Pilgrim picked up the receiver, answered the call then waited for the person on the other end of the apparatus to speak. He was greeted by the soft tones of the killer,

"Why hello there my old friend, how are you? You fucking clever ex SAS bastard! I'll bet you don't feel so bloody clever now, feeling a little bit worried are we? Well you bloody well should be, you pair of clever bastards. I'll never forget that ride back in the car with you two keeping me company for as long as I live, what a pair of wankers. I never realised I was with such a pair of losers, oh and what a lovely girl Julie is." Here the kidnapper laughed,

"You tried to keep her secret, I tell you what she made a lovely ride, a bit spirited at first but after a beating she took the prick alright." Pilgrim really was trying to control himself, although it was becoming more and more difficult by the minute, as each piece of filth rolled out of the man's mouth; Pilgrim could not take any more, so he quickly butted into the man's ravings.

"Come on you Prat, get on with it what is it you want in exchange for the girl?" Once again the assassin laughed a cold blooded laugh before he answered the question,

"You must know what I want and I know I'll get it, I want the bodies of you two lying out in front of me. I don't see that as a problem do you?" Pilgrim answered with out thinking about it.

"No I don't see that as a problem, we'll cooperate with any demand you make as long as the girl is safe. If we find she isn't you'll die a much worse death than your poor sister! That's a promise." The killer on the other end of the phone burst out laughing then proceeded to ridicule Pilgrim and Chip.

"Ooh you really sound macho when your angry, is that supposed to frighten me? Just remember wankers I've got the girl, I can kill her or I can let her live. Its how the mood takes me really for I can guarantee you will come for me, whether or not she's dead or alive. Now you know the three thick thugs from the mansion followed me here. No doubt they have just called you and let you know where I am, so I'll look forward to seeing you. Isn't it awful dealing with clever crafty Moses? Bye bye now, oh one word of warning please be careful, I don't want you to die too easily; I love the chase before I kill!"

The purr of the dialling tone told Pilgrim that the killer had put the phone down, Pilgrim was sure the northerner was aware of the pain he was causing; now he was waiting for them to come and get him. Pilgrim exchanged information with Chip as they made there way to the designated appointment of death.

Pilgrim drove there this time for a change, again his troubled brain ran through the sequence of events over the last few years, what troubled him was, his incarceration that diverted his life in the same way a train is moved into a dangerous siding! Remembering clearly how happy he was with his life before this cruel diversion, how earnestly he prayed to God in the loneliness of his prison cell for help, now have these same prayers brought me to this nightmare scenario?

These two parts of his life do seem to be travelling side by side as if inextricably linked. This entire story is even making *him* curios, he just cannot wait to see where it takes him; to the grave or to a new life? Only time will answer this cynical personal question, surprisingly his own journey in life was accompanied by Chip his friend; whose life also traversed unfortunately in a similar manner as Pilgrim's! For most of the journey there they were both silent until Pilgrim spoke, goaded into commenting by his fears for the future!

"You know Chip I beginning to think, I am one of the unfortunates of life, as for being pardoned by the authorities for the murder I served time for; I'll believe that when it happens. It has all been solved too quickly for me to accept, that it's a reality!"

Chip shook his head as he spoke,

"I can understand why you are adopting that attitude, I have to say all my troubles are ones I have manufactured for myself, when I think I was willing to gamble for a piece of illicit love was pure madness, I certainly can't blame anybody but myself. I understand that your problems were beyond your control; in fact your whole situation is very sad.

By comparison I have nothing to complain about, I miss my wife more and more as each day goes by which reflects a punishment in itself, but it's a case of just getting on with it. As for this escapade with our Julie, this is without doubt absolutely horrendous, we can only hope for the best!"

Both men lapsed into silence while the BMW soon threaded its way through the evening traffic; amazingly in no time at all they were sitting outside the crematorium; in an unlit small lay-by. They were able to see the building was very isolated, a perfect setting; the killer had a macabre sense of humour wrapped around his revenge!

Pilgrim stopped at the kerb outside the wrought iron gateway leading into the apparently isolated establishment. Switching his car lights off completely, and then waited for the thugs from the mansion to meet them while sitting in total darkness.

The street lights were of a poor quality, throwing shadows across the street, and with bushes lining either side of the roadway, it was fuelling their imagination; making it more difficult to control their inner fears. Pilgrim and Chip sat for fifteen minutes, no one appeared.

"I think it's about time we moved in, I can't hang about here any longer!"

Pilgrim nodded as he answered,

"Yes let's get to it."

They locked the car then stood for a moment studying the darkened area in front of them,

"What do you think? I think the driveway is a no no, some how we have to get right round the back."

Pilgrim thought for a second before he replied.

"I don't know if I agree completely with that, let's face it; its bit obvious not to use the driveway. So I think I ought to use the driveway while you work your way around the back as you said. We can't stay together under these circumstances that's for sure, do you agree?"

Chip nodded as he answered,

"Okay I'll go for that, just be very careful when you go up the drive old friend, just remember he wants us dead."

Pilgrim nodded with a grim smile on his face, then the two friends split up, Pilgrim watched Chip climb a low fence then disappear into the greenery. While Pilgrim pressed his key to unlock the car to open the boot, then moving away a layer of blankets to reveal five hand grenades; with more ammunition for the machine pistol; Pilgrim loaded his pockets with the weapons, shut the boot down then started the long walk up the drive.

Pilgrim's heart was pounding, he was careful to keep to the side of the driveway in the shadows of the heavy foliage either side of the narrow roadway. Fortunately it was a moonless night, which helped his immersion into the surrounding greenery. He was glad that he'd decided to wear his lightweight running shoes; at least they enabled him to move in silence or run like hell, if he had to!

The disconsolate ex-jailbird carried the machine pistol down at his side swinging it as he walked at a steady pace; suddenly he felt a light piece of string tighten along his body at stomach level. He knew instantly what it was, stopping to very slowly move back from the cord, which was strung across the roadway. He reached out to feel the cord once again then very lightly allowed his fingers to move along the string, following it to its place of origin at the side of the road.

The string was attached to several hand grenades set at different levels guaranteeing to catch an unsuspecting victim. Pilgrim expertly disarmed the booby trap then carried on only this time he was more careful, the trap reminding him of past dealings with the tricks of hunting the expertly trained Patriotic Party members. Gradually the shape of the crematorium came into view, Pilgrim stopped for a moment to study the target area; but could not help wondering how Chip was progressing?

* * *

Chip moved quietly as he could through the dense undergrowth, unfortunately there had been a small shower prior to their arrival, which made the leaves of the dense foliage give him many unwanted mini showers; especially when he tripped head over heels on a tree root. Making Chip wish he'd gone down the driveway, instead of stumbling through the undergrowth like bloody Charlie Chaplin!

He smiled at the thought of telling Pilgrim his inner thoughts and how his good friend would take it, for they both knew Pilgrim's route was far more dangerous; knowing the ex SAS man was extraordinarily more capable of coping with any booby traps the canny Northerner might have laid. Chip's heart was now pounding so he felt for the snub nosed little pistol he carried in his hip pocket, patting it then feeling reassured by its company.

Now Chip could see the outline of the main building, he moved slower with more stealth, straining his eyes to see any sign of Pilgrim, moving forward he felt a slight tug on his legs, thinking it was once more a bramble which had joined the kidnapper's army, to make things as uncomfortable as possible for him; so he pulled at it with his right leg—violently, Chip met more resistance than he bargained for, which caused him to stumble then fall forward into the wet undergrowth. Chip began to swear vehemently a split second before the booby trap exploded.

A piece of metal tore through Chips clothing embedding itself deeply into the flesh on his shoulder. The pain from the wound washed over him like an electric shock, which then exploded into a painful ache. Leaving his whole body numb for moments until Chip was able to pull himself together, realising how lucky he was falling over causing him to miss the main blast; but at this moment he did not feel very lucky, no matter how many times he repeated to himself through gritted teeth.

"I am bloody lucky. I am bloody lucky." As Chip sat up he could feel the blood oozing from the wound, he cursed the man responsible for this work of the Devil. He tore his shirt from his back then slowly ignoring the pain tore it into shreds, bandaging it tightly around his arm and shoulder as neatly as he could.

Then struggled to his feet surveyed the area as well as he was able to, in the stinking dark—in the stinking fucking undergrowth that surrounded him; swearing oaths he never knew he was aware of. Then standing against a tree supported by his good left arm, he breathed deeply several times trying once more to regain his composure so he could proceed; in just a little more careful manner.

Chip thought about Julie inside this isolated building, and how terribly frightened she must feel, he felt an overwhelming hate towards this man, a depth of hatred he hadn't felt since the fatal confrontation with the pimp.

His thought's skipped through his head tumbling over one after another like clowns in a circus, sometimes making sense but most of the time the hatred corrupting good reasoning; but ensuring Chip's resolve to finish this bastard who'd declared war on him and his kin.

Chip wondered how on earth he and Pilgrim would ever get to this golden chalice, or even if they would ever survive this particular encounter. He heaved a deep sigh shaking his head at the same time thinking aloud,

"I don't see any future for either of us at the moment, but never mind it's just a case of day by day dear Lord, or in this particular instance minute by minute! Hoping he looks after the good guys, especially those who were wounded in the pursuit of justice" Chip pushed all these thoughts from his mind; he then decided to move a bit closer to the main part of the building.

There was not a light on anywhere but it was strange how clear he could see. Chip didn't know if it would be advisable to move around to the front of the crematorium, but thought he would wait until he heard movement, or received a signal from his colleague.

* * *

Pilgrim was now very careful after finding the hand grenade booby trap, he kept moving along the driveway at a steady walking pace, Pilgrim suddenly stopped—he was sure he could hear a low moaning sound; standing perfectly still—allowing the quiet to deafen him. Yes, definitely a moaning noise, he moved very slowly towards the disturbance as it grew louder.

Pilgrim could not believe his eyes, there in front of him stood a big man whom he recognised from the mansion with a nickname of Keyboard. A rope thrown over a tree pulled up as tight as it would go around this man's neck, pulling him to his tiptoes holding him in a suspended position, whereby he just about managed to stand on his tip toes; Keyboard tried to speak but being hardly able to breathe was unable to.

Pilgrim studied the man and the state of him in detail, tracing the rope behind Keyboard knowing there would be a booby trap attached to it. Pilgrim moved around to the back of the suspended man, for there in front of him were three hand grenades connected to the rope used for suspension.

He knew that there was also a danger of further explosive devices, but decided to take a chance and go for disconnecting the ones he could see. Pilgrim's hand was starting to tremble, this continual pressure of disconnecting explosive devices was beginning to get to him, especially after he'd completed the disarming of these latest deadly traps; Pilgrim started to gradually let the thug drop down to the ground until he was free.

The heavens opened, it poured with rain as if ordered by an observing enemy, coinciding with the man's feet as they touched the ground. Pilgrim watched the individual closely, Keyboard stood for a few minutes rubbing his neck; and when he did speak it was only a croak, the result of the tight rope around his neck.

"I fought I was done for mate, that evil bastard has a mind like the Devil."

"How did he manage to get you into that position?"

The big man croaked an answer,

"I suppose it's because we're not used to coping with his sort of

villain, all this cloak and dagger business, it's all bollocks I'm used to honest villainy!"

Pilgrim had to suppress a smile, it was quite funny until Keyboard brought his hand up close to his eyes to study the terrible wound with the blood pouring from the palm if his hand, but now his eyes were accustomed to the darkness and driving rain; Pilgrim could see quite clearly the wound pouring with blood, causing Pilgrim to ask what had happened to it,

"For fucks sake what happened to your hand?"

Keyboard again croaked an answer,

"That nice little man shot a hole in it then laughed as he did it, saying it would stop me from handling a gun, the prat didn't know I'm left handed!"

Pilgrim was disgusted at such an evil spiteful act,

"He really is a sick man, hold on I'll have to tear a bit off my shirt to bandage it."

Pilgrim carefully pulled out his shirt from his trousers, then tore a strip from it then wrapped it around the wound fairly tight; hoping the bandage would stem the flow of blood.

"Do you want to make your way back to your car or come with me?" Keyboard's face was suddenly thrown into a grimace as he spoke.

"I'm coming with you mate, I don't think you have noticed the body of my mate in the dark; it's over there. He's done for him; I want that bastard real bad."

"I don't know your name but I think you know mine."

Keyboard nodded as he spoke,

"Oh yes—I know yours is Pilgrim, Mine's Keyboard, one thing is for sure I will be your friend for life. Where you go I will follow mate to watch your back. We were sent here solely to protect your mate's sister from the crazy killer, but we arrived a little too late to stop her going off with him. So we were only able to follow him to this poxy place."

When he'd finished speaking Keyboard unconsciously looked at his injured hand in the dark, then drew in a deep breathe and slightly shaking it as if trying to lose the pain he was suffering.

Pilgrim could see even in the darkness the pain and discomfort the wound in Keyboard's hand was causing him.

"Are you sure you want to come along with me? I think it would be better to go somewhere to have the hand properly attended too."

Keyboard nodded again as he spoke,

"I've never been so sure of anything in my life mate, I want that bastard real bad."

Pilgrim shrugged his shoulders as he answered,

"Well okay, but please do as I ask you, as you've already seen there's booby traps all over the place. Fortunately we haven't far to go. The building is just a few yards but there's bound to be a final trap, it would suit this guy's sense of humour."

Pilgrim turned slowly making his way towards the crematorium, cursing every one and every thing. The top of the list was the rain then the northerner followed by God whom Pilgrim accused of getting him into this "fucking predicament," for as Pilgrim saw it if the Lord above had not taken his wife he wouldn't even be here.

Keyboard followed listening to this quiet acidic torrent of accusations not uttering a word, but managed a slight grin through the pain and the added torment of rain. Until Pilgrim held up his hand asking in a whisper for Keyboard to stand perfectly still, Pilgrim thought he could see the glistening of a cotton twine running across the path about waist high.

The rain was easing off a bit, the two men looked pathetic figures in the dark, both men soaking wet through; standing like statues both uncertain of what was lurking in the night, waiting for them to make the wrong move.

"Do you see it Keyboard? Just ahead of us waist high, the bastard has a present for us I'm sure of it."

"You're right, I can see it, and fuck knows how you managed to see that."

"Well I'll tell you if I hadn't, we'd both be dead that's for sure, if you look carefully to the right the twine runs up to something in the trees. That means it would have hit us head high. Absolutely fatal, he is without doubt an evil clever bastard. We're lucky that I've dealt with them for a couple of years, but nothing as bad as this."

Keyboard shook his head in disbelief,

"What are we going to do, can you handle this or do we go around it?"

"That's what he wants us to do, for around there is another one and you can bet your sweet life it's bigger and worse than the one we have here. So I think I will handle this one Keyboard, but first I would like you to at least kneel down; just in case I blow it—if you know what I mean!"

"I know exactly what you mean, so I wish you good luck for I think you're gonna need it."

Key board knelt down in the wet and the mud to study Pilgrim's movements hoping they would not be dealt another deadly blow.

Keyboard froze as he watched Pilgrim slowly move forward to run his hand carefully along the twine to its detonator. The rain started to fall heavier prompting Pilgrim to curse once again; but finally his gently groping hand finding the source of the booby trap explosives. Even Pilgrim was surprised at the amount of hand grenades waiting to blow his head off.

The way the twine was so delicately tied to each grenade made it impossible to disconnect, so Pilgrim stood frozen to the spot his brain racing trying to make a decision. Then carefully turned speaking to Keyboard in a low voice pronouncing his words slowly with emphasis,

"We have one hell of a problem, they are connected in such a manner it's impossible to disconnect so we have to detonate them; and hope there are no more around to blow us away."

Key board in the few passing seconds had stood up from his kneeling position, to face Pilgrim as he listened intently to the explanation of his dangerous observations, his face never changing to what he heard or when he answered; it remained totally without emotion.

"Okay do what you have to do, but explain to me before you do it, in detail what I have to do, I don't want to have to stand here with half my head off saying I didn't understand you."

Pilgrim stared at the big man standing by the side of him wondering whether or not he was joking or was this guy a born comedian, for it was all Pilgrim could do to stop from bursting out laughing at this straight man standing in front of him. Pilgrim nodded as he spoke

"Ok that's a deal"

The big guy smiled as he answered,

"Good that's made me feel a lot better."

At this final remark Pilgrim could not control his amusement any more he just burst into laughter, trying like mad to keep as quietly as possible. Keyboard held out his hands in front of him like a good Jewish boy as he answered,

"I thought you were never gonna laugh."

Then he also joined in laughing uncontrollably. Perhaps it was the violence or the black cloud of continual fear with no reflection of happiness, affection or jollity. Just violence and more violence, was it laughter or hysteria. Pilgrim didn't care what it was, so they stood with the torrential rain falling on their heads then dripping from their noses; plus the blood leaking from Keyboard's hand!

For a few moments more they both laughed until their ribs ached, while Keyboard was holding his injured hand close to his body covering it with his good hand; cradling it as if it was a complaining baby.

Pilgrim held his hands up appealing to Keyboard to stop the hilarity and listen to what he had to say,

"Please Keyboard just listen—what we have to do is lay flat on our stomachs, and then I will find a piece of long stick to poke at these grenades which hopefully will set them off. God willing, they in turn will cause others to explode to clear the area. So let's move to our right to carefully lay down covering our heads with our hands, while I do my best to detonate the rest of the traps."

They did just that, carefully laying down in the wet and the mud, both characters calling the rain and the mud and every terrorist born in the world names, that even made Satan himself cover his ears. Pilgrim called to Keyboard softly.

"Are you ready, I don't want you going to sleep in such luxurious surroundings?"

Keyboard smiled answering quickly,

"Yes I'm ready and I wish you luck!"

Pilgrim smiled as he started to reach up to the twine endangering their future, hitting it as hard as he could with the mundane choice of stick in his hand that had been chosen as their life saving wand; which instantly brought the result required.

Several explosions went off at second's intervals, while Pilgrim and Keyboard tried desperately to bury themselves into the soil on which they were laying. Their hands covering their heads, hearing the whistles of the shrapnel pass by their ears. Making them cling closer to God's good earth trying to wear it like a vest whilst praying for safety. The explosions stopped as both men laid still for a further few moments unsure whether or not to move, hoping the rain of metal was finished, only then did the silence also become noisy. Pilgrim and Keyboard slowly started to pull themselves up from the ground until they were standing. Pilgrim turned and spoke to Keyboard,

"Let's hope that's done the trick!"

The men moved forward slowly, their eyes straining to see into the darkness for anymore designs that would propel them to an early visit to their maker. They kept moving very slowly until the outline of the crematorium came into view; suddenly every light in the building came on illuminating the entire surrounding area.

Pilgrim with Keyboard stood perfectly still frozen in the shadows, wishing they could see into the building from where they stood; knowing that it was inevitable they would have to move across the well lit area to do just that.

"Pilgrim, he's one bag of tricks this bastard there's no doubt about that!"

Pilgrim nodded but didn't answer the obvious for he was to busy trying to work out the options he had in front of him for entering the building, but at the moment they weren't looking very good. Pilgrim wondered where Chip was, if he was safe and in good order.

"I think we ought to go to the other side of the building, I think Chip's waiting there for us; I hope."

They both moved stealthily in the shadows of the trees and the undergrowth, the edge of light from the building, slightly disturbing their vision into the darkness on their left.

Pilgrim hoped Mister Moses hadn't added to his bag of tricks in the area, by planting more little explosive surprises. With the light on their right blinding their vision, to the left lay the long dark driveway, leaving them with little hope of seeing any dangers in their path.

Their mouths were now feeling very dry especially with their movements reflecting fearful anticipation of disturbing more death traps, it all made Pilgrim and Keyboard feel as if they'd aged more in those few seconds than any other part of their lives.

As they made steady progress, Pilgrim was able to see Chip crouching on a lower roof of the building, gun in hand peering out into the woods obviously looking for him. Pilgrim and Keyboard by know were almost standing opposite Chip, only the broad expanse of illuminated tarmac stood between them.

Pilgrim eyes flicked over and around the building, wondering whether or not there were any spy holes or windows, where the enemy would be able to study them in any detail unseen. He could not see any vantage point where they could be seen by the opposition, so taking a deep breathe sauntered out from the shadows of the woods into the light, breaking into a zigzag run until he was with Chip. Keyboard shook his head in disbelief muttering.

"That guy is either very brave or very stupid! I'd like to think he's very brave. One thing is for sure I'm not staying here on my own, here goes."

Keyboard was never a fast runner, he was too big a lump for a start, but never the less he ran as hard as he could to be by the side of Pilgrim; puffing and panting, feeling very relieved he was still in one piece.

Pilgrim stood looking at him in the half-light with a big smile on his face,

"Blimey! Keyboard you are so fast I doubt whether a bullet would have caught you!"

Key board through the puffing and the panting answered gruffly,

"Don't take the piss."

Pilgrim suppressed a sly chuckle then turned to concentrate on the job in hand, calling out to Chip,

"Can you see anything Chip?"

Pilgrim saw Chip move his hand to his mouth and then lay one finger across his lips in a gesture of asking for silence.

"Hmm I think he's answered your question mate, there's something going on."

Pilgrim nodded in agreement as he answered,

"We need to get up there with Chip to know exactly what's happening."

Pilgrim started to climb the same drainpipe Chip used, after a lot of huffing and puffing, both men joined Chip peering through a roof light into the main hall of the crematorium.

What they saw did not please them too much; the elderly man who was released by them, whom they also think killed and mutilated the kidnapper's sister was standing high upon a large cross roof beam. Halfway along that main support where the old man was standing, with his hands tied behind his back to an upright beam which sprung from the crossbeam to the apex of the roof. From the upright two more beams sprung from that centre one from either side, at a fourty-five-degree angle. Julie was tied to one of them; while both of them stood on the cross support marginally safe!

A noose ran around his neck and Julie's, tied to a higher beam pulling only him to his tiptoes; while two separate ropes tied around their legs ran down to the hand of the notorious killer, seated in a chair quite comfortably enjoying a cigarette as if he were on a sunny patio of a delectable hotel. The observers realised a tug on either rope, would automatically dislodge the captives feet from the safety of the beam, leaving them suspended by their necks.

While the boys felt no concern for the old boy's predicament, they were very worried about Julie. For a few moments the boys were lost for words by what they were confronted with, Pilgrim was the first man to speak.

"I hate to say this but there's only one way to deal with this and that's for me to end up on that beam with Julie."

Nobody answered, again the silence, then Chip retorted,

"What you are saying is you gonna have to give your self up to that little shit!"

"Yeah, I don't know any other way, I've just gotta get up to Julie on that beam."

"I suppose you are gonna ask us to stay here looking through the fucking window!"

Answered Chip in too louder a voice! Pilgrim snapped back an answer,

"How the fuck do I know how he will react to my entrance, I hope and pray I will get the opportunity to kill the bastard!"

Key board groaned—

"How the fuck did any of us get into this, I'm used to putting the pressure on mugs for a bit of protection, but not all this acceptable casual killing."

Chip rolled his eyes in agreement as he spoke.

"That makes three of us, but it has to be done mate." They all scrambled down from the roof, then Pilgrim motioned to Chip and Keyboard to stay in the shadows outside, while he made his entrance.

Pilgrim drew in a deep breathe, then pushed the side door open then stood just inside the door, the Northerner turned his head to get a good view of his visitor, his face splitting into a grin at the same time.

The old man on the beam next to Julie, was amazed to see the entrance of Pilgrim; knowing this was the end of the honest fool standing just inside the door. The old man really wanted to die obviously appreciating the fact that his death was not very far away. The consequences of judgement in the hereafter, frightened him for he knew he had not been a good man; but death as a package beckoned him joyously at least it would end his pain! Looking down on the fool who stood before Moses, he knew he also was going to die very shortly with as much pain as he was in; he was going to enjoy the sadistic script being acted out in front of him at this moment!

"Well well, how are you old friend? Please do come in. Don't be stupid enough to try to do any thing clever, if I fall the ropes tied to your bitche's legs are attached to my wrists; so in the event that I should fall—will cause a nasty accident."

Pilgrim's heart was pounding so loud, that he thought that if the northerner listened carefully enough he would hear it.

"I'm aware of that!" Snapped Pilgrim!

"I thought you would be more interested in putting me up there on that beam then agree to let Julie go and leave the building." The crazed killer smiled as he stretched in a lazy relaxed manner remarking,

"I'm really enjoying this, I couldn't be more pleased than if I'd got your bollocks in my hand and was really squeezing them, but I think you're right. You definitely need to be up there on the beam with the pretty little lady down here sucking my prick!"

Pilgrim knew the bastard was really trying to wind him up and was being very successful. The aggressor spoke and broke his thoughts.

"Come over here, close to me then drop your weapons. I must warn you if I find any weapons on your body I will automatically kill the girl, so be warned."

Pilgrim dropped his beloved automatic machine pistol along with the ammunition, and then all four of the hand grenades which were hanging on his body attached to a belt around his chest. His aggressor whooped with surprise, when he saw the weapons Pilgrim had been carrying.

"A right little SAS man aren't you. Now you are totally disarmed, move right over here to me then drop down onto your knees."

Pilgrim's mind was racing; he knew what was in store for him if he didn't act quickly. An enemy of the P B P was always dropped to his knees before the traditional death shot was delivered to the back of the head by a revolver. Pilgrim glanced upward at the two on the beam.

The old man, who was guilty of killing the killer's sister, stood there a pathetic sad figure. His shirt open, his chest bleeding from deep knife wounds, his trousers ripped open at the knee with blood still pouring from the bullet wound in his shattered kneecap. His face swollen from bruises, agony and suffering written across his features, in his mind he must have been praying for death to end his misery; but most surely anticipating more pain before the final event.

Julie, she was angry and scared, angry that she was in this predicament through her own stupidity. Now she was really frightened, so frightened it took all of her self-control to stop her legs from collapsing. She had watched Pilgrim enter the building, accepting the fact that at least they would all die together, in a building that was meant for dead people and now for the dying! Pilgrim looked up at the pair of suspended hostages.

"So you've acted out your revenge on the old man, bringing you right down to their level. Remember the level you boasted that you had never gone to when you found your sister! Well now you have. You really are a clever little man."

The killer burst out laughing answering Pilgrim's jibes through clenched teeth, "Just do as I tell you otherwise the girl dies!"

As Pilgrim moved slowly forward trying to postpone this awful confrontation, his body and mind tingling with sensitivity and fear, the throwing knife pressing into his backbone. The terror of it being found caused a pang of dread to flip his stomach, the retaliatory retribution if the weapon was found on him, he knew would be terrifyingly awesome. Pilgrim suddenly realised the only chance he had left was to use the fucking knife, he could still feel the throwing knife sitting in his belt pressing into his back, knowing it was his only hope.

Many times in his past during barrack room competitions and in several frontline attacks he proved to be very accurate, but never envisaged he would ever be confronted with a scenario of this horrific calibre. Laughing and smiling and enjoying the torture that was going through Pilgrim's mind, the killer absolutely aware Pilgrim knew the execution procedure; knowing he was going to die.

This made Pilgrim make up his mind, hoping he was successful in getting to the rope in time to stop a tragedy, for he had no other chance of surviving.

Pilgrim moved as fast as he could, moving his hand slowly at first then quickly to pull the knife from his belt, with a flick of his wrist sent it hurtling towards the sick wretches neck as hard as he could.

Then throwing himself forward in the hope of catching the ropes, attached to the two people's feet that would cause them to be pulled off the beam to their death; that is if the crazed killer fell with the lines attached to his wrist.

The moments prior to the knife reaching its target, the uncertainty of whether or not it would hit its victim, in Pilgrim's eyes it seemed as if the weapon flew through the air in slow motion; amid the torture of failure causing sudden sickness in his stomach.

He managed an upward glance at the figures teetering on the edge of life and death, their distraught pale faces knowing this was a flirtation with the old scythe carrier himself. Pilgrim's eyes moved back to the victim mesmerised by the flight of death speeding towards him and he could do nothing about it.

The knife met its target spot on with the assassin dying amidst a gurgling sound and jerking movements before falling to the floor.

Pilgrim managed to grab one of the ropes then heard the sound of a fall and then the sickening sound of a neck snapping as it hit the extremity of the rope, slowly lifting his head to see who it was who died, Julie or the sick brained old man. The door burst open behind him; suddenly he could hear the sound of running feet.

It was Keyboard with Chip slapping him on the back as he watched the horrific sight of the old man dancing and gurgling on the end of the rope; fortunately Julie was still perched on the beam her face as white as porcelain too terrified to move.

As for the old man he took great pleasure in seeing his torturer die even though it insured his death, he felt his feet being pulled off of the beam as he managed to spare a thought about his maker wondering in his craze of pain, if this time he might evade the Devil and become an angel; although he didn't think it very likely! The remark from the old man out on the road that night, about asking him (Pilgrim) to remember he owed him a favour sprung into his mind, well I suppose it has been repaid; what a way to repay a debt!

Pilgrim ignored the back slapping of his colleagues holding the rope to Julie's feet tightly in his hand staring up to Julie, then starting to speak to her softly and with care. His other two companions became silent, for they also suddenly realised the emergency wasn't over—yet.

"Julie Julie! Can you hear me alright?"

Julie's answer was almost like a puppy's whimper as she answered Pilgrim.

"Think now Julie where is the ladder he used to get you up there?"

For a moment she struggled to find the words to answer—but she did,

"I'm not sure—I—I—think he threw it outside the front door."

Pilgrim spoke in a quieter but firm tone to Chip and Keyboard, who were standing beside him,

"Go quickly and find the fucking ladder, before she falls off the poxy beam!"

The two men rushed away to find the apparatus; and were back in no time placing the ladder against the rafter. Pilgrim was soon up beside Julie, holding her tightly against the upright beam with his chest; while he untied the holding ropes to the wooden beam.

With a little talk and a lot of help she was soon down safely. Pilgrim sat with Julie comforting her trying to keep her gaze away from the old boy still swinging about on the end of a rope.

The man's distorted features reaching the realms of horror, his face a dark blue and his tongue hanging from the corner of his mouth, which was wide open as if still trying to gulp down air into strangulated lungs; his neck still horrifically stretching.

The boys dreading the fact they would have to get the sadistic old prat down, to try to dispose of the two bodies as quickly as possible. Keyboard disappeared for a while, but come back to inform them that there were a lot of bodies still in their coffins; waiting to go into the furnace.

"I think that we ought to drop these two bodies on the top of the other coffins, and then pull the lever for the furnace to get rid of all of them."

Chip nodded in agreement, and then spoke to Pilgrim.

"Pilgrim please, take Julie home away from this house of horrors and leave all the clearing up to us."

Keyboard interrupted,

"Yeah and we mustn't forget my mates out there, their bodies have to be dealt with."

Pilgrim nodded in agreement.

"No doubt this is what this sick little character had in mind for us; perhaps I should not say that. I know personally the pain grief can cause, I think in the man's situation with the loss of his sister, it completely distorted his sense of proportion.

It is such a pity it had to end like this, another place another time and no doubt we could have been comrades in arms; unfortunately sometimes life can play such strange tricks on us all!"

Chip and Keyboard went about the business of collecting and destroying the evidence that would reflect this horror evening's events, as Pilgrim took Julie out of the Crematorium then into the car; that was soon heading for the safety of home. Chip along with Keyboard once again faced the darkness of the undergrowth in the rain, to find Keyboards old friends; hoping to dispose of them with the other two passengers on the furnace conveyor belt!

After some foraging around in the darkness, with the assistance of a torch they stumbled across the bodies they were looking for; unfortunately they did stumble across them. It caused Keyboard to trip falling full length into the black pit of soaking wet under growth, Keyboard like a gentleman swore no more than once; for he was feeling quite remorseful for the loss of his good friends.

Both men as big as they were found it difficult and very hard work carrying the bodies, which were a dead weight in every sense of the word! Keyboard struggled with his bad hand and Chip in pain with his damaged shoulder.

At last they arrived in the back room of the crematorium then stood surveying the controls of the furnace; it was something Chip was not enjoying. So he suggested to Keyboard they proceed to also bring all the other bodies through to this side of the furnace.

After a lot of pushing swearing and pulling, then unavoidably having to study the horrific facial expressions of the corpses they handled, also going through the pockets of the same hapless victims; they were more than pleased to come to the end of this awful task.

"I'll tell you what I think, we will have to make a pile of furniture in the middle of the floor, set it alight with the help of some paper to burn this place to the ground; it's the only way we can be sure we've left no trace of our visit."

Keyboard nodded, the task with his injured hand was making the work as difficult as climbing Everest. Keyboard and Chip worked as hard and as quickly as they could, until they were satisfied the large pile in the middle of the floor was sufficient. Keyboard pulled open all the cupboards managing to find a large tin of highly flammable liquid polish; which they used to pour over the collected pile.

For just one moment Chip opened his mind and his eyes, using them to glance around the scene that he and Keyboard had created, the line of coffins waiting for their turn to move into the furnace; with the added dead bodies as silent passengers lying on the top of the casks.

Grotesque commuters with twisted faces, with dangling limbs covered in a patchwork of dirty red bloodstains, the coffins uncomplainingly accepting the extra cargo on a ride to a man made Dante's inferno.

Chip changed his line of vision to the bonfires they had built in the centre of the room, chairs, cupboards they'd pulled off the wall, papers hymn books, notice boards thrown into a huge pile eccentrically balanced.

Again Chip moved to the control panel pulling the switch, to start the caravan of death on its way to a spiritual destiny. Keyboard at the same instant threw a flaming torch onto the pile already covered in the flammable liquid polish unknowingly supplied by the caretaker, which burst into flames at the touch of the torch.

Both men stood as long as they dared, watching the hungry flames spread up into the roof then along the dry timber area, making sure before they left the building nothing was going to be left; only then did they leave as quickly as possible. Chip climbed into his BMW while Key board jumped into his newly acquired Jaguar. Both cars tyres spat dirt as they accelerated away from the location of nightmares!

CHAPTER 16
Strangers Can Sometimes Be Friends

Pilgrim put Julie to bed when they got home, kissing her tenderly tucking her fully clothed in the bed warm and safe, turning out the bedroom light then thanking God for her safe return against all odds.

He then went into the kitchen raking around for a pencil and paper, when he found the paper with the pencil he scribbled some instructions on it for Chip and Keyboard; then went into the lounge to find a comfortable armchair to await their return.

Pilgrim was dozing in the chair when his two comrades arrived to tell him all was taken care of, placing Pilgrim's throwing knife along with his machine pistol on the coffee table in front of him speaking and explaining to Pilgrim details of their activities at the crematorium at the same time.

"We torched the whole building, we could not risk even a minute trace of our visit there, also Keyboard told me how it was on the journey along the drive; in fact he said he didn't know how you came through it. He seems to think you're some sort of super man! I happen to think he's right; also I don't know how I will ever be able to thank you for saving my sister's life."

Pilgrim's eyes were cast down on the carpet while Chip was speaking, he slowly lifted his head to look into Chip's eyes, waiting patiently for him to finish talking before holding his hand up to maintain Chip's attention. What Pilgrim really wanted to say was this,

"I appreciate your gratitude and your friendship, but in the second when the knife was flying toward its target, I was caring about Julie, a deep care, in a way that I never did before. Possibly it was something that I've felt for a long time and never knew; maybe it was all arranged before my wife's death.

To slot into place the moment I knew my wife was dying, realistically I could have felt this way for along time but pushed it out of the way because I was frightened of hurting my family. I am of course referring to my imprisonment and then when you and I were released from prison meeting your sister when I did; it was not a good time for me to let my feelings run uncontrolled.

So what I'm saying to you is old friend, I'm madly in love with your sister and up until now was unaware of it. The whole exorcism at the crematorium was unknowingly in pursuit of saving someone I was and am madly in love with."

That was what Pilgrim wanted to say; what Pilgrim actually said was with an acknowledging smile of modesty on his face was,

"I just did what I had to do."

Pilgrim received from Chip a broad smile as he answered,

"Okay, if you're happy thinking that but me and Keyboard know differently, for if it was not for you I think we'd all be ashes at this moment in time old friend, so thanks once again."

Pilgrim wiped his nose with his sleeve before speaking again,

"It's over thank God, also you have one more chore to complete; and that is you will have to take Keyboard and your good self to get your shoulder fixed. So go to our S.A.S doctor at a safe house address—he won't know who you are, please don't offer any names, he won't ask for any, the address is in the kitchen, mention only my name. Please take poor old Keyboard to the docs before gangrene sets in and he looses his hand."

Chip disappeared into the kitchen then moved towards the front door, Keyboard joined him as he walked out of the flat. The door slammed and just for that moment Pilgrim sat staring at the weapons on the coffee table in front of him, recognising that these weapons normally associated with violence were over the last few hours, responsible for bringing him so close to this woman lying in the bedroom asleep. These entire past events making him see quite clearly, that he was and had been for a long time madly in love with Julie.

Pilgrim never dreamt of anything or any body, the nights work had exhausted him physically and mentally. His wife or future plans appertaining to the hunt for the golden chalice did not disturb the coma like slumber he entered into, for this was an escape from something he knew deep down inside he and Chip should never have got themselves entangled with.

He was now fearful at what would come next in this pursuit for what he thought was pure fancy. Never—the—less they had accepted gold to step into an ongoing nightmare, that he couldn't see the end of.

Shrouds of sleep cocooned Pilgrim's mind and body keeping away dreams or images from the past or future, until he felt the touch of warm succulent lips and a hot tongue pushing into his mouth!

Then greedy eager hands of love unbuttoning his shirt and pushing their way around and over his body, Pilgrim's eyes started to flicker open seeing a blurred vision of the love he'd found a few hours before.

His heart beat faster his whole body tingling; groping lustfully for the curves and the cavities of Julie's body. Feverishly kissing and groping each other's bodies they fell to the floor, Pilgrim stood up, his six foot four broad muscular frame scooping Julie into his arms to carry her into the bedroom, placing her gently down on the bed, kissing and fondling then undressing her. Clumsily undressing and falling naked upon Julie's warm unclothed body, kissing and cuddling.

The kiss this time for them both was not lust alone, unrequited love that had festered—while neglected, existing whilst being ignored and now it was bursting free; like red hot lava bubbling and pouring down the side of a volcano.

Freed from its depressed origin, hugging each other's naked bodies desperate for each other's love; till Pilgrim fed himself into the wet causing Julie to groan with joy. They reached their sexual destiny clinging to each other as shipwrecked lovers, lost in a sea of hostility. The honesty of their love gave way to the extremities of strain and tiredness.

When Chip returned with a treated shoulder and a bandaged Keyboard, finding the bedroom door open he stood at the foot of the bed smiling, as he witnessed and covered up the two exhausted lovers lying above the covers naked as the day they were born. For he realised they were lost in a deep sleep, still clinging together, immersed in love and adrift in paradise.

When Chip was satisfied Pilgrim and Julie were safely asleep, while he and Key board had received medical attention to their superficial wounds; Chip suggested Keyboard fetched the box from the Paddy's Jaguar for them to look at.

So Keyboard did just that, placing it on the table in front of Chip then sitting down by the side of him to drink the tea Chip had made. Chip with Keyboard sat forward on their chairs to get a closer look at the newly acquired article that was the cause of their burning curiosity.

Both men studied the box in silence, Chip's hand reached forward to touch it carefully; running his hands over the lid then feeling the ornate black ebony pattern set into the darkened polished mahogany.

Keyboard picked it up to look closer at the lock beautifully set into it's ornate surround, as he did his eyes started to blur strangely so did Chip's. Keyboard had gulped his tea down, but Chip had only finished half of his.

Chip knew what was happening and felt violently angry but knew there was nothing he could do, he then slumped back into the armchair like Keyboard; to fall into a deeply induced slumber.

The early morning sun awakened Pilgrim, spilling through an adjacent window immersing his sleep—ridden features in its warm bright rays. His eyes opening slowly to rove around the unfamiliar surroundings; then gradually very gradually pieces of the jigsaw from the night before tumbled back into his mind.

Pilgrim sat up in bed, leaning on one elbow to study closely the features of the woman who had dramatically re-entered his life, only to steal his heart away so suddenly and effectively.

The full horrors of the visit to the crematorium ran through his mind like a recurring nightmare, bloodstained bodies; hideously distorted faces stricken with fear and death. The vision of the old man swinging like a pendulum on the end of the rope, with his neck stretching to the length of a swan's, still fresh in his mind.

Pilgrim knew all this and more would never be erased from his memory; if he had lost Julie to the evil schemes of the fascist; then this whole package would have been too much even for his mental strength to contain. For he knew no sane man could ever evade the persecution of his own conscience.

The sudden emergence of Julie into his sad life was an event worth celebrating with champagne. All these thoughts raced through his mine as he continued studying Julie's attractive features, he could not resist stroking her hair; inadvertently bringing Julie into his waking world.

She stared intensely at the face looking down at her, then she remembered the immediate past, slipping her arms around Pilgrim's neck; pulling him to her, clasping him tightly to her body. Not ever wanting to let him go again, thinking this night of love was an isolated incident; that would end with this day.

Pilgrim sensed this desperation in the embrace of her arms, whispering comforting loving words in her ear.

Only for Julie forced to mentally deny promises of any future with her lover, envisaging a loving wife forever hovering within that guarded arena. Pilgrim realised certain details needed to be explained, carefully—gently pulling Julie's arms from him; then placing his fore-finger across her lips, after wiping away a lonely runaway tear.

Pilgrim slowly and articulately related to her the sorry tale of the last twelve months of his life; adding to that the feelings for her surging through his mind and body. Pilgrim paused before delivering his final rhetoric;

"Julie what I'm struggling to say is, I'm in love with you and have been for a very long time. Whether or not you see me as a,"—Here Pilgrim paused struggling, trying to find the right words.

"Or will you accept me for a long time partner is something I would like to know."

Julie lay silent while Pilgrim's story unfolded, absolutely stunned. She could hardly believe that her wildest wish had come true, not of course the tragic death of his wife; but a situation occurring that would bring the love of her life to her as flotsam on the tide after a storm. Happiness oh joy! Flowed through her very veins, in a way only complete fulfilment of love can bring.

As Julie in her exuberance kissed Pilgrim again and again and again, gasping out words of passion, promising words of divinity from here to eternity. Joy oh joy! No more lying awake in the early hours, feeling so lonely she could have cried a flood to drown London, but all that would pass as once more they consummated their love. Again to drift into that other Eden, he holding her so close she could hardly breathe, to then sleep the sleep of innocents, blessed by surrounding smiling angels.

The morning light fell across the carpet from the open window, the traffic noise inheriting the responsibility of the cock's crow to herald the start of a new day. Pilgrim stood up from his bed shaking his head, grabbing and gathering his underwear and clothes thrown in a pile in the heat of passion from the night before. Half-dressed and suffering from joyous after effects from a night of love, but still half a asleep he felt the need for a cup of tea.

Pilgrim stumbled from the bedroom into the adjoining lounge to be confronted by four large aggressive looking characters, who he had never seen before in his life. But at that time at that moment, his brain churning digging at memories from the night before, remembering the night with the early morning of love and exhaustion which made him smile. He still could not find any thing available in his memory or reasoning to justify the presence, of four thugs!

Standing in front of theses guys bollock naked, the smile was misunderstood by the men holding the guns; but Pilgrim's smile was noticed as a welcome sign to them, making Pilgrim think perhaps they were not the bad guys after all.

"Well are you gonna explain yourself or are you going to carry on staring at my bullocks with silly grins on your faces."

The largest and the eldest looking of the four cleared his throat to speak with the tone of authority in his voice,

"No I assure you the last thing in the world we're interested in is your bollocks young man, I and my colleagues are Knights Templars; we have watched you for a considerable amount of time. Very much aware of your efforts to try and secure the Holy Grail in your war against the northern assassin; and his cronies. We are Knights Templars—people like us have for centuries acted as keepers of the Holy Grail; continually guarding against gangsters like you who work for Satan!

King Richard The Lion Heart, brought this holy symbol back from the Holy land, when he secured Jerusalem from the clutches of the infidel; then handed it to the English section of the international army of Nights Templars for eternal safe-keeping. The real reason for King Richard's kidnapping was they wanted the Holy Grail, fortunately at the time; the Templars possessed the Holy Icon.

So generation after generation inherited the duty, and willingly took their turn to hide and protect this sacred powerful symbol. Until one man—just one man after all those years down the centuries, decided to proposition shadowy characters from the dark side of life; turning into a traitor for the promise of mere gold which by comparison to the Icon is meaningless!

So that in a nutshell is how we lost this holiest of holy, after all that time; I am led to believe you spoke to the man concerned at the place you call the mansion."

Pilgrim stood studying the orator as he spoke, a tall distinguished looking character with sharp features with slight hair greying on the sides of his head. He still exuded an air of steel in his personality, but Pilgrim guessed he was a just man; but nevertheless a determined dedicated individual! When he finished speaking, Pilgrim gave this speaker an answer,

"Well that was a pretty good history lesson especially for this time in the morning; and yes—I did speak to that individual. Right now where do we stand—please before you answer that, I would like the opportunity to dress; then make a cup of tea. While you explain to us the way it all has to be, for I'm sure that's what you're going to do."

A half smile came across the face of the man standing opposite him,

"Yes of course do that, but do not bother to look for any weapons, they were all collected then carefully stacked on the hall table and are now securely guarded. You may have them back when we leave!"

It wasn't long before the four captured parties were sitting fairly relaxed in the lounge, ready to listen to terms by their captors. Pilgrim did managed to speak to Chip who was very upset about being drugged the night before, but they spoke about these characters in private. Pilgrim relating to Chip what the Knights Templar had told him of their history, both arriving at the same conclusion; that if these guys were the real genuine article then they would readily submit to their demands.

Accepting of course they were within the realms of general decency, both agreeing they (Pilgrim and Chip) at the moment were tiring of this living in a world of lies and killing. So here they all sat, ears tuned to the friendly exchange of ideas, to allow everyone to be free of this extraordinary situation surrounding them.

Pilgrim could not believe the way they had managed inadvertently to acquire the Grail, the fact that it was in the Paddy's car was astonishing; everyone sat and participated in small talk while Julie made more tea. Pilgrim sat with his own thoughts, running his eyes over the people sitting in this forum.

The notion of Keyboard driving the Jaguar back from the bonfire last night made Pilgrim smile; I bet he was tickled pink driving a car home that was owned by the bastard who blew a bloody hole in his hand.

Pilgrim's mind wandered away from Keyboard, which then trundled back to his days tracking the party members, suddenly remembering a similar case to Keyboard's; an act of happy revenge which didn't quite end up the same way. Julie was just handing out a cup of tea to Chip when Pilgrim shouted.

"Bloody hell! Listen to me everybody, the bloody Jag, I'll bet its booby trapped!"

The room was suddenly silent for a second then everybody spoke at once, then in that moment Pilgrim realised how hampered they were; caught up in this web of good guy characters. The elder of the armed men called for silence, then asked Pilgrim the question they all wanted to know.

"How do you know its booby trapped?" Before he spoke Pilgrim looked at his wrist watch as he spoke,

"I don't but its Patriotic Party procedure, something they do just in case they lose they win if you know what I mean."

The elder rubbed his chin as wise men do when they don't know the answer; he then addressed Pilgrim with words that were spoken slowly with deep thought

"Well I'm afraid we're in your hands young man, what the hell do we do?"

Pilgrim was quick to respond, showing concern for the clock ticking away the time,

"The answer is simple, get one of your men to walk by—drop a coin then drop on his hands and knees to pick it up, at the same time have a good look beneath the car to see if there is anything questionable under there." The elder gave the order to the youngest man to do what Pilgrim had suggested, so the chosen party quickly left the room. If there had been a clock ticking on the mantelpiece then the occupants of the room would have heard it, clearly!

The young man soon returned; more than a little nervous when he gave the answer to the question everyone was waiting for, in his oh so cultured sounding voice,

"Yes there is a package taped to the axle of the vehicle, of course what it is I'm not sure but there is certainly something very dangerous looking under there."

The young man was pleased to melt into the back ground of the circle of associates all looking very alarmed. Pilgrim winked quickly at Chip, who immediately nodded then they both sat back, wondering what this little crew would do about this man sized problem.

The sage of the group knew instantly the answer; he looked over to Pilgrim as he spoke,

"I'm sure you know the answer to this problem, I think we will leave it all to you. First I must tell you what you have to do to disentangle yourselves from this Satan's web, for I'm sure that is exactly what you want to do. You will be invited to attend a party, which by the way is due within the next couple of days.

Please attend then leave the rest to us, during the course of the evening you will know when we are about to make something happen, also you will know when to leave very fast. As for the bomb in the car problem, I'm sure you can handle it far better than us."

The entire group had started moving to the door as the man was speaking, notably one of them was carrying the box that was found in the Jaguar. As the last of the group was about to close the front door, one of them who up until this time had been silent throughout the entire meeting paused to speak,

"Please do not follow us, the people you met are kind and very gentle, the people you will meet if you follow us will be very different!"

Pilgrim held up his hand to catch the attention of the departing stranger,

"Before you go, could you answer just one question?"

The stranger stopped in his tracks then hesitated before he answered.

"I will if I can."

Pilgrim drew a deep breath then blurted out the question, he was burning to ask,

"What actually is the thing you all came here for? We really thought we were just participating in someone's flights of fancy."

Again the stranger hesitated before answering but this time his face adopted a more serious expression.

"This question I really shouldn't answer, but I will. This Holy artefact is the most powerful of holy earthly goods in existence; it can be used for good or evil.

One thing is certain, once it has touched your life, you will never be the same again; certain things within your life will change forever.

To get really close to it would be like lifting back the veil from the fourth dimension, as for the changes in your life I know they have already started to happen. I'm sure your little crew are not bad people just sadly misled, so because of that nothing untoward will happen to you; only good happy things! I must go now but I wish you all well."

He closed the door carefully; once again the flat was silent for they were alone. Just for that second Pilgrim and Chip and Keyboard and Julie stood quietly pondering on those parting words of the stranger. Chip broke the peace by clearing his throat before speaking softly,

"All I can say to that is, only time will tell."

It was a strange few seconds of silence that followed, for each and everyone in the room knew profoundly that in their hearts; they would never be the same people again. Chip looked to Pilgrim for an answer to the question he was about to pose.

"Pilgrim you know more about this, what do we do about the problem with the car?"

"There's only one thing we can do and that is notify the police, I know an old Patriotic British Party pass word we can use which hopefully will convince the authorities it is a genuine warning. What about you Keyboard, did you wear gloves when you drove the Jag last night?"

"Strangely enough—Chip lent me his gloves mainly because of the injury to my hand; so that's a healthy let off."

Pilgrim sighed in relief as he answered,

"Well at least we have no connection with the vehicle as it stands, other than to make the phone call, obviously that will not be from here; that's for sure."

Chip with Pilgrim followed by Julie grabbing Pilgrim's arm (obviously never intending to ever let go of him again) left quickly, to make the phone call from a box a long way from Julie's flat, Pilgrim made a call, attempting to change his voice to suit the occasion.

Keyboard stayed behind in the flat, he felt it was strange how quiet the flat had suddenly become. Nevertheless he enjoyed the peace and quiet, but certain aspects of his life were worrying him. One, he still had not contacted Tobias at the mansion; for Keyboard was very aware that he was paying his wages but he wouldn't phone him without speaking to Pilgrim and Chip First.

By nature Keyboard was not a treacherous man; for he was deeply indebted to his two newly found friends. Then he remembered something else, when he got out of the Jaguar last night he found two articles. The bag containing the object that was taken away by our Scottish friends, but—there was also a small suitcase.

He placed the small suitcase under the hall table; he thought, I suppose everyone took it for granted that it belonged to Julie. His thoughts wandered away from the bag in the hall, to find himself thinking about his association with the people at the mansion; an affinity he was not entirely happy with.

Oh he knew he was grateful at the time to old flat nose for the job, but now he felt different because of pressure from a different quarter. The girl he'd been living with objected strongly to him associating with the criminal fraternity.

They were her words not his, they amused him because they sounded a bit posh. Pointing out to him he was now thirty-two the relevant fact being, another long stint in prison would not only steal more of his life; but also would cause their relationship to come to a full stop forever; poor old Keyboard could still hear her words ringing in his ears.

"Why don't you get a proper job or start working for your self, just don't keep mixing with those losers."

Keyboard didn't know what to do, he could not believe how virtually overnight his life was now so complicated. He looked at his watch knowing Pilgrim Chip and Julie had been gone for over a half an hour, by now they should be on their way back from the telephone box. He suddenly spoke aloud,

"The bag the bloody bag, I wonder what's in it? Knowing my luck its most probably packed with Semtex."

Keyboard went out to the hall then stood looking at the suitcase under the hall table. He decided to take the plunge, stepped forward grabbed the handle taking it into the lounge in quite a resolute manner, then placing it on the small coffee table in front of his armchair; he then settled down to sit comfortably staring at the possible rogue container.

There wasn't anything outstanding about the case other than it was an old battered thing which had seen better days. The hopeful hero leant forward reaching out with his left hand pushing the catch causing it to flick up, the shaking right hand of Keyboard then reached forward to push the catch on the right also causing that one to flick up.

The lid was now ready to lift up; pangs of fear ran through the robust frame of Keyboard. All the past twenty-four hours of fear and horror were still very fresh in his mind, motivated by the chilling respect for the man that created all the pain and humiliation; in fact more than he had ever experienced personally at any one time in his life.

Throwing caution to the wind, overcome by curiosity Keyboard lifted the lid of the battered suitcase. What greeted his eyes was an astounding sight, a sight that his criminal mind had dreamt of all his life.

Successfully committing the big crime, then retiring to Bermuda, to spend the rest of his life in shorts and sandals; well here it is—a case full of fifty pound notes not exactly a million pounds but at least a half a million—a fucking half a million! Keyboard thought aloud again,

"I am very tempted to do a runner; unfortunately I owe my life to Pilgrim and Chip. So I will have to sit and wait, bloody typical of my luck all the filth I've had the misfortune to mix with; then just at the best moment of my life I have to find someone decent to work with and to make it worse I have to be honest!"

Keyboard sat and waited for his new found comrades. They entered the room chatting to each other in a contented way; the door was opposite to where Keyboard sat. The three of them stopped talking as they noticed Keyboard sitting in silence staring at the contents of the battered suitcase; Chip was the first to speak.

"Where did you find the money?"

Keyboards broke his gaze on the money to look up at Chip as he answered,

"I forgot all about it, I found it in the Jag then placed it under the hall table last night with the other box the Templars took away."

The sound of police cars began to fill the area; the additional noise of loud speakers asking for people to evacuate their premises, for an unidentified bomb had been discovered. Keyboard looked away from Chip to look at Pilgrim.

"You made the phone call then?"

"Oh yes they will take care of everything I'm sure of that."

Pilgrim sat down on the settee; Julie sat next to him. Chip sat in the armchair, directly opposite Keyboard. Pilgrim sat forward as he spoke,

"What do we do with it now?"

Chip looked across at Pilgrim and winked at him, Pilgrim picked it up instantly,

"Well" said Chip. "Me and Pilgrim have already received half a million from Toby at the Mansion, so there's only one thing to do and that is for you to pick it up Keyboard and take it home, that way we'll all be square!" Keyboard's face lit up but then a look of mistrust crept over his face.

"You're winding me up."

Chip smiled as he spoke.

"We're not winding you up mate we really mean it!"

Keyboard was quite overcome by the sincerity of Pilgrim and Chip.

"Do you know the slags I've been mixing with would have cut my throat to get to that, I just don't know how I can express my thanks for letting me keep this pile of money."

At last Keyboard thought I have something that will keep my girlfriend happy. A shadow seem to fall over Keyboard's face as he spoke,

"One problem only one problem, I still work for mister happy at the mansion, people don't walk away from him and live. At one time it wouldn't have mattered but now I have this special person in my life everything is different, it's an opportunity to turn my back on all the villains and crooked pigs; long sentences, and short sentences plus the stinking smell of prison cells. I want to walk away from all of it."

This sudden venomous tirade by Keyboard took everyone by surprise. Pilgrim felt for Keyboard, appreciating the predicament he was in.

"So this woman you've met has made quite an impact on you, enough to make you want to change your life."

Keyboard started to nurse his hand again, Julie was concerned,

"Is your hand hurting you again?"

Key board nodded before he answered,

"Yeah yeah, I need more pain killers but never mind about my hand, what are we gonna do about those lunatics in Grantham?"

Chip and Pilgrim were again taken back by this new outburst.

"Why are you saying that, you've never spoken about these people like that before?"

Keyboard slumped back in his chair, heaving a big sigh at the same time. Julie placed a glass of water and two tablets on the coffee table in front of him. Keyboard thanked Julie, then he sat forward again threw the tablets to the back of his throat followed by gulping down the water.

Keyboard paused to glance around at the faces looking at him now, knowing they were now filled with curiosity; eager for him to explain his attitude to satisfy their morbid curiosity. The Nelson look-a-like with his hand now ticked into his shirt then proceeded to relate the true story about the mansion.

"The meetings in the temple they're the stuff nightmares are made of. Groups of up to twenty people, all dressed in black. Nearly always leading a goat on a piece of string, along with the goat and a doped naked young girl; they all use to go straight up to the temple. We would hear hours of chanting, plenty of screaming; and I mean screaming. As for the poor old goat we never knew what happened to that because it was never seen again. I must say also as for the young doped girl, we were always unsure if she came down again with the main party, or if she ever did."

Chip pulled a face of disgust as he spoke.

"What you're saying is they are practicing Devil worship."

Pilgrim nodded in agreement as he spoke,

"That's what the man called Moses told us!"

Chip stood up,

"Please excuse me for I'm very interested in what you have to say, but I'm curious as to what's happening in the street."

Chip walked out on to the balcony to survey the scene in the street, there were several people in blue overalls lying on the ground under the car, Chip could see several pairs of feet protruding from under the car but nothing was happening. He rejoined the company to hear Julie speaking for she was really fascinated by the words of the man with the bandaged hand.

Pilgrim studied her features with loving eyes as she spoke, Chip could not help but notice it and it brought a smile to his face.

"Well Keyboard how have you tolerated all this evil? Surely just knowing and seeing it all happen for the first time would be enough for most people?"

Keyboard looked at Julie as if she were a bit simple,

"A man like me mixing with the people we do, only money motivates the likes of us, you belong to a different world. It is almost a different planet, money and only money; no principals no morals, no loyalties Julie only money. So you see we didn't give a shit if they were shagging dogs up there in the temple, the man was paying big money; that and only that was the bottom line." It was Chip's turn to heave a huge sigh before he spoke,

"I understand that, in fairness we're all a bit like that if we're honest, what on earth has changed you to such a degree so suddenly."

Keyboard shook his head,

"Oh it's not a sudden change; the whole set up has been knawing away at me like a mouse at a piece of cheese. Of course you two boys with your caring attitude and camaraderie helped me to start believing I could really step out of this cess-pit.

The final straw of course was when you said keep the money—keep the money! I think the time has come for all three of us, to free ourselves from this web of evil."

"The man from Edinburgh said he had it all arranged; he inferred that an agent of theirs would be on hand to tell us to leave when the time came."

Keyboard still posturing like a Nelson look a like, wagged the forefinger of his left hand as he spoke.

"Do you know what I think; I think we are all going to be invited to a full moon party!"

Julie was now really all agog at the mention of a full moon party and all it conjured up in her mind.

"What on earth is this, a full moon party?" Keyboard suddenly became more than a little uncomfortable when Julie asked this question.

"Come on tell us."

Urged Chip eager to know as well as Julie.

"Don't worry about Julie she's a big girl now.

Keyboard smiled a naughty boy smile that highly amused his listening audience,

"Well I'll tell ya—perhaps I'm wrong but it's a bloody big orgy, they all arrive about eleven in the morning and make for the ballroom, everywhere in that Satan's temple is this drink a particular type of drink that sends them all sex crazy. Again the room fell into silence while they all thought about what had just been said, only to be broken by Chip.

"How do you know all these details Keyboard, did you ever participate?"

"Good gawd! No I didn't!"

Answered keyboard highly indignant at even the suggestion,

"You know all about the hidden cameras in every room of the house, me and the rest of old flat nose's crew were the one's who manned them. So we knew everything that went on!"

"So you think we are going to be invited to a full moon party."

Asked Chip—trying to keep a straight face. Keyboard nodded his head certain of what he was going to say,

"That sick man thinks it would be a way of rewarding you for getting rid of the Paddy."

A shadow fell across Julie's face,

"I certainly hope you don't accept!"

Pilgrim gave Julie a quick cuddle and spoke reassuringly,

"Quite possibly Julie, we will most likely have to string along with it for a while, so please don't worry. Any way this is only supposition on

Key board's part, I really doubt this will happen; for I think there are far more sinister occurrences to be concerned about than the one being referred to!"

Chip went to take another look at what was going on in the street appertaining to the booby trapped car, as he did he saw the blue overalled bomb disposal expert get out from under the doomed car then sprinting away down the street. Chip moved quickly back to his company in the lounge to warn them of the immediate danger.

"Come on! Down on the floor behind the settee, Moses has fooled the experts, they've run for it!"

Julie Pilgrim and keyboard with Chip quickly moved to sit behind the settee just in time. The car must have been blown twenty feet into the air. Every window in Julie's flat was blown out, all the glass blown across the lounge with pieces sticking in the settee protecting them. The group sat silent for several seconds after the blast, Chip was the first to move followed by the other three.

"What a mess! All this glass! "I think this is entirely your fault Keyboard!"

As Julie finished speaking she winked at Pilgrim then carried on.

"After all you did park the car there!" Keyboard saw the wink and carried on with the kidology.

"I think you're after my money, well this may cause me to sulk for a while" Pilgrim laughed adding.

"I think it's a small price to pay for a life saved don't you Chip."

Chip nodded smiling.

"Oh yes, where ever Mister Moses is now he must be laughing his head off seeing the cream of the British army bomb disposal units, running down the road as fast as his little legs could carry him!"

As they all returned to more comfortable seating, Pilgrim addressed

Keyboard,

"I suppose it's time for you to find out what is happening at the

Mansion Keyboard?" The little group went suddenly quiet, realising once more they would be stepping into the fearful unknown!

CHAPTER 17
Nemesis Opens Her Eyes!

Pilgrim with Chip listened intently to Keyboard's phone call to Tobias, promising to give a detailed report on his return. On the journey to the mansion the three men away from Julie were free to discuss the horrors at the crematorium, as for Julie she was moved away to a safe secret address; which made all the men feel very happy, knowing this time Julie was secure!

The nightmare experience of that evening left indelible impressions on their minds and spirits, the event forging an unbreakable bond on the trio; a bond they knew was so strong it would last to their dying day. They also decided unanimously to deny all knowledge of the Templars; or the contents of the box that they took away.

Pursuance of honest and deep conversation brushed away the miles, for soon the car swung into the long drive leading to the Victorian mausoleum. Keyboard wondered who if anybody had taken over from his friend flat nose, for him his sudden reappearance at the mansion seemed strange; as if he now worked for a different team. Relinquishing links with his former colleagues, perhaps Keyboard thought this was all in his mind. Nevertheless his loyalties certainly lay in a different direction to when he left, a point he will have to remember not to show, it could cost him his life.

As for Pilgrim and Chip they too wondered where they went from here, maybe Tobias will give them a new address to visit in pursuit of the dream of Tobias's life. What about the Templars? When would they appear on the scene or are they already here? It seemed to Pilgrim it was all a package of whys and wherefores, which only time would reveal the result.

As for us three, well it was a case of playing it all by ear. Chip glanced around the car conscious of the silence that had fallen amongst them as they neared the Victorian pile of bricks, the fascination of not knowing what sort of reception they would receive; or maybe hidden hostility only to emerge at a time when they were more vulnerable.

Possibly a heroes return; for a bunch of fools who should have known better, than to get tangled up with this sort of evil. His thoughts traversing across the sequence of events and people they'd come into contact with over the last few weeks.

The only one his heart bled for was the assassin's sister; he felt she was an innocent bystander unfortunately dragged into something she knew nothing about. He knew well the sort of girl she would have been because of his association with other girls of her trade; it used to be his job. To think I used to be one of the men known as the filth or the flying squad, better known in London cockney slang as the Sweeny Todd!

So here I am again he thought working for the worse sort of filth than before, thank God I've got Pilgrim with me. Pilgrim's facial expressions whilst in deep thought went from grim to amusement thinking about the night of nightmares. Hoping events waiting for them at the mansion would not unfold into a similar scenario.

The car stopped at its usual place, by the steps and under the stone portico supported by the ornate stone columns. As they were about to get out, Keyboard nudged Chip.

"Ere you'd have thought they would have been plenty of dogs around to protect this place, don't you think so?"

Chip looked at Keyboard as if to say I've got better things to think about, but he answered him just the same,

"Do you like dogs then?"

Keyboard grimaced as he answered the question,

"No I hate them, one bit me when I was a kid. I was just thinking about it; when I first came here I expected lots of dogs! My dad always said dogs were no good because they were born again alcoholics, condemned to drink water for the rest of their life!"

Chip looked at Pilgrim and they both burst out laughing!

"Keyboard you should have been a bloody comedian!"

Chip turned off the engine leaving the keys in the ignition, then joined the other two lads who were still laughing, to grab the small amount of luggage they needed for an overnight stay. The door swung open as usual but this time fresh faces met them to take away what they carried, then they ushered the visitors into the hall.

Pilgrim and chip were surprised to see Tobias waiting for them, greeting them like long lost sons. Tobias's face was displaying the best grin they'd ever seen in all their visits. This caused the same thoughts to swarm into all their minds, an insecurity; which made them feel very uneasy.

The boys tried to ignore the uneasiness twisting their minds and stomachs, casting concerned glances at each other—when they could. This feeling was worse than turning up at Christmas without a present for the invalid child!

Pilgrim's mind raced through past events, assuring himself it would be impossible for anybody to know the full story; other than the people who were actually there. They followed Tobias into the dining room where the table was set for lunch, their host pointed to where he wanted them to sit. There were empty spaces at the table; so Chip wondered who else was expected.

Tobias joined them, with help from a bespectacled weasel looking character; who managed to wheel him into his place at the table. Tobias surveyed the group sitting around him, Keyboard Chip and Pilgrim. Keyboard looked very uncomfortable, obviously anticipating nothing but trouble. Keyboard—Chip thought, would never make a good poker player; Tobias who was wearing a beaming smile opened the conversation.

"Please forgive me, for our other guests will be late. Never mind while we wait a small aperitif would be more then satisfactory, Ronald will do the honours."

The four men watched the weasel with the glasses on the end of his nose, dressed in a white shirt with a black tie matching his black jacket and dark pinstripe trousers. Nodding his servile head to each recipient as he poured the red wine, it was obvious to Pilgrim this was a man whose spirit had been crushed. Pilgrim was wise enough to know that crushed subservient men when given the opportunity; turn into dangerous ruthless enemies.

The dining room door opened revealing two men who entered; one about fifty years of age the other around forty. Conservatively dressed, in fact after studying them closely you would say they were from the Bible belt. Pilgrim recognised one of them instantly. It was the man with the soft Edinburgh accent, that he met the night Chip drank the drugged tea while Pilgrim went on walkabouts in the Mansion during the dead of night.

His thoughts raced questioning how this particular man was called a Judas by his fellow guardians of the Grail. As for Pilgrim he mentally recalled the facts concerning the runaway Templar, as the newcomers drew their chairs up to the table wearing large smiles. Tobias introduced Alex, the man Pilgrim had already met, the man with him was called Gerard; both men were from Edinburgh.

Tobias looked around the table, guessing his company were anticipating a few words from their host, so he did just that—he lifted his glass as he spoke,

"Gentlemen I would like you all to join me in a victory toast, a toast only made possible by the ingenuity and tenacity of these three men sitting with us. Chip, Pilgrim and Keyboard! Bringing to me an article I have chased all my life. Only in my wildest dreams could I ever have hoped for such a successful turn of events. Gentlemen I give you the toast. Chip, Pilgrim and Keyboard!"

The other two men echoed their names, and then downed the wine.

Pilgrim, Chip and Keyboard were now squirming in their seats, totally dumbfounded by the words they were hearing. Did this man in the wheelchair sincerely believe that they at last managed to capture this elusive Grail? Dark glances were passing between them; the other guest's well they were completely relaxed bubbling—full of confidence. The man Pilgrim met on that eventful first evening in the mansion looked over to Pilgrim and smiled as he spoke.

"How are you Pilgrim I've heard a lot about you and your friend. Such dangerous escapades, it's a wonder you both came through it all unscathed!"

Pilgrim nodded smiling along with Chip; Pilgrim shot a glance at Tobias as he spoke to Alex,

"I never thought I'd ever see you again, so this is a nice surprise." Tobias eyes widened as he heard Pilgrim's remarks and was quick to interject.

"If you remember I assured you Alex was in safe company."

Pilgrim smiled as he answered.

"Perhaps such a large house with darkened corners can fire ones imagination, and you Tobias are a man that never ceases to surprise me; that's for sure."

Tobias accepted these words from Pilgrim as a compliment, Pilgrim didn't care whether he did or not. He was beginning to feel really pissed off with the general approach of his host.

Chip began to sense Pilgrim's changing attitude and was becoming more than a little concerned, trying to quieten him by giving Pilgrim a kick under the table. The conversion around the table paused into a loaded silence, while everyone watched the food being served, Pilgrim was still working himself into a lather feeling it was time to clear the air; so he addressed Tobias when he spoke.

"You obviously know what we had taken from us."

Tobias cleared his throat before he spoke then paused for a moment just to put a little drama into his words,

"Oh yes we know that alright, what you are not aware of is we were watching the whole sequence of events from start to finish. Fortunately it all worked out very nicely for me, thanks to you!"

Here Tobias stopped to take a deep breath, to then carry on speaking,

"You see the problem for all parties without doubt; was the killing capabilities of the assassin. Nobody else was professional enough to be able to neutralise this individual. Now, when you and Chip entered into the scheme of things, we were astounded by your expertise, we stood back to watch the action.

The arrival of our Scottish friends in such an open manner, made it easy for us, all we did was to take the Grail from them; painlessly of course." With these last few words from Tobias you could almost hear the guns spitting death! Our trio, were staggered by this revelation, so for a few moments were lost for words but in those fleeting seconds, the memory of those words of warning from the serious looking man, who paused to speak to them at the door of their flat; rushed into their minds. Pilgrim knew it was a really heavy warning, so when the time comes for this Nemesis to appear; Pilgrim hoped they weren't around. Chip was the first to speak,

"So you saw the horrors of that evening?"

Tobias sort of half nodded as he answered,

"Not myself in person as you might say, but my long serving employees saw nearly all of it. Then when it became more relaxed, well the Grail was there for the taking, so we took it."

Chip shook his head in disbelief,

"So were we just used, as a couple of fools to stand in the front line?"

Tobias frowned as he answered making Alex and Gerard to start feeling a little uncomfortable.

"I didn't consider you fools, I thought of you more as heroes on my behalf!"

It was Keyboards turn to shrug his shoulders as he spoke,

"Heroes or fools? Perhaps that's what this life is all about!

Tobias gave Keyboard a withering look,

"I don't know about that rubbish—but I'll tell you this, I would not mind being called a fool if a half a million pounds was paid into my account!"

"Who do you mean, exactly; the three of us or just me and Pilgrim?" Tobias was quick to answer,

"The three of you of course, Keyboard played an important part in the affair suffering as much as any body."

Here Chip joined the conversation,

"I'm sure Pilgrim like me will not have any argument with that, Keyboard was and is a very important part of the team."

Pilgrim nodded in agreement.

"Well," said Keyboard, "let's fill our glasses and drink a toast to Pilgrim and Chip"

Pilgrim thought this particular moment was the right time, as far as he personally was concerned to ask a very poignant question.

"Tobias how did you know I was an innocent man?

Again the man in the wheel chair smiled that knowing look,

"I am able to delve further into people's lives more than any official organisation; I pride myself on exacting investigations. As for your particular case, I know the people concerned and am very much aware of there questionable activities. You were due to your expertise, getting too close in your investigations to the truth for a certain Mister Right Honourable Etherington.

So this cabinet minister, with his massive financial clout managed to corrupt the two officers whom you are now aware of, all this I discovered when I was deciding whether or not to invite you into my employment. I have been assured that your innocence and pardon with the help of particular friends in the M I 6 agency is absolutely assured!"

Pilgrim's brain was beyond the stage of answering in any coherent form, so he sat quiet for once in his life; which made Tobias's smile grow even wider.

Keyboard sat there looking and listening, completely stunned by the news he'd been rewarded with half a million pounds, plus the information about Pilgrim!

"Excuse me Mr. Tobias; I'd like to say a few words now if I may. I haven't in the past been well known for my verbal ability. But this time I have to make an effort, first I'd like to thank you Mister Tobias; then I'd like to tell you about these two characters sitting here. In my time I reckon I've worked with and for some real hard mean men, but Mister Tobias I'm glad to say these two men are my friends because they are the coolest and the hardest I've ever met in my life."

Pilgrim and Chip really felt embarrassed by this praise from Keyboard, Tobias with Alex and Gerard were grinning from ear to ear. It was time for Tobias to deliver another toast to the two heroes. The toast was heartily drunk, and then it seemed that in no time at all, the small talk like the dinner was over; and it was getting late. Pilgrim and Chip along with Keyboard thanked Tobias for his hospitality, then wished them goodnight; the weasel with glasses showed them the way to their rooms.

Keyboard sat in his quarters looking around the room, noticing his overnight bag was at the foot of the bed. He then heard a tap at his door, when he opened it Pilgrim was standing there.

"Come on mate you're not sleeping here!"

Keyboard nodded, picked up his case then followed Pilgrim out of the door. Chip was waiting for them in his room, Pilgrim sat down on the bed while he spoke to Keyboard in a very low tone of voice,

"Now listen very carefully Keyboard, the simple reason we have stayed alive is because we never sleep at the same time. Always always, one of us must stay on guard! I'm certain the only way the three of us will survive this night is to maintain the same system; one of us must always be on guard! Keyboard I must explain to you the drill, I like to think what I would do in their position if they wanted to kill us; so the first thing I would plot is a scheme to split us up.

So here's the drill, at no time under any circumstances will you leave this room without telling both of us! For what will surely happen later on this evening, one of your former cohorts will come knocking on the door asking you to accompany them for a drink; that's the sole reason I want you to take the first guard until two am.

When it happens, and it will as sure as night follows day, then you will wake us up, for the next on the agenda will be the Templars, they will liven this old place up about three in the morning."

Keyboard looked at Pilgrim with a surprised look on his face as he spoke,

"Whatever makes you think all this is actually going to happen Pilgrim?"

Pilgrim looked at Keyboard with a very serious look on his face.

"Keyboard when we were in prison I never did any thing else in my rest time other than read. When they told us they were Knights Templars, I knew we were facing a serious military opposition. Also if Tobias's employees were stupid enough to kill the men that left us that morning, then I'm afraid Tobias has a very serious problem on his hands!"

Keyboard nodded answering,

"Okay, I'm not going to argue with that, let's face it if you're wrong we'll still be alive and that's the name of the game."

Pilgrim looked at Chip as he spoke,

"What do you think Chip?"

"I go along with everything you say Pilgrim!"

Pilgrim showed Keyboard where he wanted him to sit, which was the corner that the door opened against. They then stuffed the bed with pillows from Keyboard's and Chip's rooms, proceeding to make up two sleeping positions on the side of the bed hidden from the door; first of course they found the hidden cameras as in all the rooms they were each given to sleep in.

Pilgrim and Chip settled down to try to hopefully grab a few hours of sleep, Keyboard sat behind the door holding Pilgrim's favourite toy; the mini Uzi micro sub machine gun making him feel very confident!

Pilgrim was tired, but under the circumstances, the new revelations from Tobias, caused his mind to stir these facts around and around in his mind. He felt this entire saga was an unforgettable experience.

As for my promised redemption from the pit of iniquity that he was thrown into due to other people's lies, it seems the truth was now about to spill out into the honest light of day; like a bowl of clean clothes from a washing machine!

That might now create a reincarnation of happier days; like a phoenix rising from the ashes of my former destroyed life. It was all very hard to believe, very hard to believe! With these last thoughts slipping through his mind Pilgrim managed to fall a sleep.

Keyboard under different circumstances would have found sitting in the dark until two in the morning a very tedious duty. In fact it would have been doubtful even if he would have accepted the suggestion! Now of course, things were different, for the first time in his life he'd found someone who needed him. Didn't sneer at his slurred East End accent, or that he'd done plenty of bird. (Prison)

After all Keyboard thought, what a journey his life had been. A long series of protection rackets, robberies, prisons. It just had to come to an end, his girlfriend was right. It was only a matter of time before he came in front of a judge who would really want to bang him up for twenty years.

Everything would be gone then, that would be the end. There was a matter of a further half a million pounds that would dovetail nicely into the first half million pounds. The only important event on this agenda was getting out of this place and staying alive while he did it.

Joyous day dreams tumbled through Keyboards waking brain, enjoying the thought of spending a little of the money, not too much mind. Now with a bit of luck he with his girl friend could be laying on a beach in the Bahamas, pushing his hand down his sweetie's bikini fondling a sweet fanny. The thought of that alone kept Keyboard entertained for quite a while! After several hours had passed, the daydreams were interrupted by a whispered voice calling his name accompanied by a soft but impatient rap on the door.

"Keyboard open the door! The boys have invited you down for a drink at the party, it's an orgy! You'll love every minute of it!"

Keyboard could not believe the accuracy of Pilgrim's reasoning. He walked to the door then muttered to the person on the other side of the door in a soft voice,

"Hold on I'll be right out!"

Turning quickly he moved to the area where Pilgrim and Chip were sleeping. He shook them firmly,

"Pilgrim come on we have a visitor!"

Both of them jumped up and were quick to gather their senses. Pilgrim moved over to the door followed by Keyboard and Chip. Pilgrim spoke in a whisper.

"Chip we need to get that arsole in here! Keyboard tell him to come in while you dress!" Keyboard opened the door a couple of inches as he spoke,

"You'll have to come in while I dress."

The conspirator walked in and Chip instantly jammed his Glock 17 into the back of his head, while Keyboard quickly closed the door. Chip told the man to stand perfectly still otherwise he was going to die. Pilgrim spoke to him quietly but with a very firm voice,

"Now move to the side of the bed and kneel down with your hands behind your back."

The hostage started to whine thinking he was about to go into the execution position,

"It's nothing to do with me I'm just the messenger, Tobias sent me!"

"You lying little bastard you know exactly what's going on!"

The man knew he was in deep trouble which motivated a confession,

"They're all down there; they're going to kill all of you wankers!"

Chip picked up a cushion to place by the side of his gun to kill the sound. The man thought he was gonna die and started to whinge,

"For fucks sake what sort of people are you!"

Keyboard bent down so his face was close to the hostages as he answered,

"The sort of people who don't like being set up by fucking killers like you!"

The three comrades were suddenly astonished to see Chip was now the victim with a gun stuck into the back of his head by another member of the Satanist's gang!

The main lights of the room were switched on so they could see the wheelchair bound Tobias, sitting within an opened wall panel at the far side of the Bed. It was obvious this was a hidden escape door, for the three friends were now the prisoners of this weirdo.

The chair bound lunatic smiled as he spoke, all three of the captives noticed instantly he was a different character. This man was a sneering arrogant individual who now felt he was completely in control of his own destiny, which was most certainly the path to rendezvous with Satan!

"Did you really think you would be able to walk away completely, to broadcast to your friends my personal affairs? How do you think I knew so much about your past? You see I was the man responsible for organising the scheme to put you in prison. I was the man who enjoyed the absolute destruction of your life, then I have enjoyed building it up again and now I will take great satisfaction in killing you!

Me! I was the man who was washing all my criminal profits by acquiring government contracts, with mister Etherington the minister working for me; none of you pious Christians can refuse the promise of big money. All of you are so easy to corrupt, my Lord Satan rules over all of you; I have proved it. It is unfortunate you will all die; the good point about it is you will all die in the payroll of my blessed ruler Satan!

Before I dispose of you, I will allow you to witness the ceremony to initiate the using of the Holy Grail; so that my Lord Satan can cast his spell upon what was once God's, but now will belong to Satan's people!

Manacle their hands then tie their feet so they can only shuffle, also tape their mouths; then bring them to the temple. Before I go to prepare myself for the ritual, I must tell you this; I have a surprise for you I'm sure it will please you."

When he finished speaking, the power filled evil man burst out laughing; it was the worst sound that ever came from a human's lips. Then a button was pushed and he disappeared in the hidden lift sinking into the depths, his evil laugh echoing through the building; lost below as quickly as he had appeared.

The three companions were forced to accept their fate, well for the time being anyway. They were dragged down the corridor partly pushed and partly dragged, and sometimes punched into the temple. The gloom of the atmosphere with the only light bursting from a central domed panelled glass window, helped to throw dancing shadows over the Satan's worshippers completely naked, their bodies glistening with sweat in the half light.

First glance at the Satan's servants dancing to some ritualistic music was at first awesome, then after several minutes sickened by the swinging sweaty breasts and plunging penises. Some of the participants were old men and old women, which as a sight was absolutely abhorrent! When their eyes became adjusted to the poor light, they cast their eyes to the altar on which stood a dwarf, with the goat's head on his shoulders, cavorting on the surface of the altar in time to the beat of the naked sex performers before him!

The participants gradually gathered intensity with the beat of their sick sexual movements, building to a pinnacle then sudden absolute silence and stillness fell across the temple. It became obvious they were all waiting for something or someone to appear. The parting words from the lunatic in the wheelchair had slipped from their minds completely. They could sense the thugs who held them, also felt nervous, sorely affected by the drama acted out before them!

Again a panel slowly slipped open at the back of the altar and the man in the wheelchair emerged still naked, his shrivelled limbs and body an ugly sight, on his head he also wore a hideous horned mask of the goat. He sat in the wheel chair naked, on his left side were two naked assistants, holding a naked woman in their grasp who seemed to be either in a trance or she was drugged.

Her face also covered by a mask depicting a beast of the field, Chip and Pilgrim remembered the story Keyboard had told them of the suspect killing of the young woman they used in their past Satanist rituals. Suddenly they wondered if this was what they were going to witness, the slim bodied beautiful naked woman stood perfectly still as if unaware of all what was around her.

Then one of the naked assistance snatched from her head the ugly mask and they to their horror recognised it was their beloved Julie, they thought she was safely tucked away from this evil world.

The three struggled to free themselves from their bonds, but their accompanying captors knew their pathetic struggles were useless, watching them and enjoying their horror filled faces; while they gazed lasciviously at the curves of the naked young woman. The girl was then moved closer to the altar then assisted to lie down on the black marble slab while the two who had brought the girl in moved away to bring large candelabras.

These contained black candles, which they proceeded to light amid a sudden communal chant from the naked observers. The chanting started in a quiet slow tone then gradually like the dancing gathered speed becoming louder, and louder. Through the gloom, Pilgrim, Chip and Keyboard could see the wheelchair man struggle to stand who was then supported by his companions, Chip along with Pilgrim struggled as hard as they could to snap the binds that held them!

Pilgrim thought his heart was going to burst with the effort his muscles striving trying to break free, but it was hopeless. Again the chanting stopped, then Tobias was offering to his Lord Satan a ritualistic prayer; as he was mumbling the words his hands was drawing a long pointed knife from its scabbard.

The onlookers now silent, while the mad cripple's voice was getting louder as if he was working himself up to a frenzy; which heightened their fear for the girl's safety! The three friends realised the lunatic was going to use the deadly looking knife on Julie and there was nothing they could do about it but watch.

The knife was gradually raised above the prone body of this beautiful girl, the chanting from the assisted cripple stopped; Tobias was still held firmly in the hands of these two naked men. Silence suddenly fell across the temple while the hand holding the long pointed knife stayed poised, held high above his head over the sacrificial victim; only the sound of muttering from his lips broke the silence.

So they waited, frightened to even breathe, fearful of the awful act to be committed; praying to God for his help, for only he could.

It was as if their prayers were answered for several shots rang out across the temple and two of the men by the side of the cripple fell to the floor. The crippled freak holding the knife fell backward as the other man holding him let go, for the temple was suddenly full of armed men.

Not caring who they killed but shooting at random. One of the gangsters by the side of Pilgrim also fell to the floor; causing the group who held them captive to make a run for the door. Tobias in his wheelchair pumped his hands as quickly as he could, moving him backward into the secret lift from which he sprung earlier.

Two of the Knights Templars were soon at their side releasing their bonds, one of them muttering,

"Quickly get the girl out of here the whole building is going to be blown apart!"

The trio moved to Julie's side, Pilgrim ripped a velvet ceremonial cover from the wall to throw it over Julie; gathering her up into his arms almost in one sweeping movement.

The three friends moved as quickly as they could back to their rooms to gather all the suitcases, they slammed their door on entering then grabbed all their personal belongings, but first laying Julie on the bed; she was till in a heavily drugged state! Key board blurted out a comment as they moved feverishly.

"I will never deny the presence of the good Lord again."

As Keyboard finished speaking there was a loud knock at the door followed by a voice they recognised. Pilgrim and Chip glanced at each other; it was the serious man, who had stood at the door of their flat; warning them of an act of serious retribution against these Devil Worshippers. Pilgrim walked over to the door, opened it slightly and peered through the gap; and then opened it wide to welcome in and greet the Templar.

"We are really pleased to see you!"

He shook hands with Pilgrim speaking words of assurance as he did,

"Don't worry our soldiers are swarming everywhere throughout the building."

Chip asked the Templar,

"What's going on?"

He wore a very grim look on his face as answered,

"When we leave with the Grail, every one of our enemies will be dead and this building will be burnt to the ground. You three men, with the young women should leave now!"

Pilgrim Chipboard and Chip looked at each other deciding instantly as one to leave immediately, Keyboard almost ran over to pick up his overnight case, Chip called out to him to leave it.

"Leave everything I've a feeling it's gonna be difficult to get out of here!"

Keyboard looked over to Chip nodding in agreement. The Templar gave Pilgrim his keys to the BMW, as he did so he told him it was a hundred yards up the drive. He offered Pilgrim his hand and Pilgrim shook it, so did Keyboard and Chip. As he turned away he stopped to speak again to the three of them.

"You will never see me again; as I told you before your lives will change— in fact the movements in your lives have already started."

The Templar disappeared out through the door; the boys stole glances at each other and were soon following the path of the Templar down the corridor; Pilgrim struggled onward with Julie in his arms.

As they progressed along the corridor towards the staircase a further explosion rocked the building, clouds of smoke and dust swept along the corridor. It caught them up enveloping the trio completely, causing them to splutter and cough; Chip and Keyboard held their handkerchiefs over their noses and mouths.

When they came to the main stairway it was just starting to disintegrate, their descent became more dangerous with each step. Explosion after explosion rocked the building, causing large pieces of falling masonry which seem to chase them down the stairs; adding wings to their feet.

A final dash through the front door, then a further two hundred yards gallop, which now seemed more like two miles; Pilgrim was beginning to tire badly needing assistance from his two friends to carry Julie. When they finally arrived back at their car, the group of escapees quickly tumbled into the safety of the vehicle; only sparing backward glances to witness the ongoing collapse and destruction of the entire mausoleum.

As Chip pushed the accelerator to speed away from the cloying hands of Satan's people, not a word was spoken by his perspiring breathless passengers; fortunately Julie was still in a comatosed state. The three men did not spare a thought as to how the Satanists were surviving; in fact they were acutely aware their days were numbered!

Tobias sat in the basement accompanied by Ronald the weasel in front of the open lift door that quickly rescued him from the attack in the temple; he was of course still naked as he was born. Heavy explosions rocked the building one after another, sounding just like artillery gunfire; enormous pieces of masonry came crashing down into the hallways and corridors. Tobias shouted at the weasel ordering the sly little character to carry him up the stairs, the weasel moved away from Tobias, then stood laughing at him. As he spoke smirking,

"What do you think I will do, get close enough for you to nearly strangle me again, I can see no problem with the stairs. This time you will have to find your own way up!"

Tobias sat staring up at the man scampering up the stairway, his face like stone watching the laughing employee as he ran up the collapsing staircase, the weasel stopped for a moment to gaze down at the cripple in the wheelchair.

This rich and powerful man that could only sit and watch and wait for the concrete beams falling and the fire erupting around him, trapped in his chair like an animal in a cage; a solitary isolated figure gradually becoming horrifically smashed to pieces and then buried half dead—lost in the falling rubble.

The weasel stood watching this macabre scene laughing, enjoying this destruction of his former employee, just managing to reach the top of the staircase then scramble onto the landing only to be caught in a hail of bullets from the soldiers of the Templars; killing anybody associated with Tobias Friedman the evil Satanist. Hell bent on wiping these people from the face of the earth, almost as if they had never existed!

CHAPTER 18
Everyone Has What They Want—Or Have They?

Morning broke and Keyboard was restless sleeping on the settee, as for Pilgrim he was enjoying a contented nights sleep with Julie in his arms. Keyboard found not only the settee uncomfortable, even though he was grateful for the temporary sleeping accommodation, but he could not get the money out of his mind.

Everything he'd ever wanted was now in his grasp; he couldn't wait to see his beloved girlfriend. It was seven-o-clock, time to get up to boil the kettle, for he was gasping for a cup of tea!

He was joined by Chip who came stumbling in, half asleep who also needed a cup of tea, the two boys chatted away to each other drinking their tea, the catastrophic events of yesterday purposely dropped from their memories.

The three boys had decided not to mention in any way the nightmare of how Julie was used and abused, fortunately the drug that was fed to her turned out to be a saviour, because Julie was absolutely oblivious to any of the unfortunate occurrences.

The sound of clinking teacups enticed the two lovers from their nest, and then the four of them sat in the lounge drinking tea discussing their future. Only Chip was quiet, undecided what he was going to do with the rest of his lonely life, Julie sat casting concerned glances in his direction knowing he felt out of the general run of conversation, strangely absolutely unaware of the occurrences in the Satanist's temple.

Julie sorted out the three men to wash their hands again like small boys, for breakfast, getting them to lay the table; then butter the bread to also making a fresh pot of tea. While she cooked a substantial fried breakfast, when it was over, finished and eaten, Pilgrim with Keyboard volunteered to wash up. Of course Keyboard with his wounded hand opted out of all the work, amongst a lot of derisory personal remarks from Pilgrim and Chip, Key board playfully answering; said he would do it next year which gave all of them an idea that they would discuss later.

Julie sat talking to Chip, when the front door bell rang; all of them froze realising it could be friend or it could be foe. Julie jumped up saying,

"I'll answer it."

Pilgrim and Keyboard peeped out from the kitchen, like small boys spying on their elders, straining their ears trying to recognise the voices they could hear. They heard Julie say to the person at the door,

"Would you wait a minute please?"

Then they heard her footsteps from the hall into the lounge, Julie entered directing her words to Chip.

"There's a woman at the door asking for a man called Horace!"

Chip knew instantly who was at the door and could not get there quick enough, the occupants of the flat heard a few words spoken followed by the sound of the front door being slammed.

They, Pilgrim and Julie with Keyboard following, rushed to the balcony to call out to Chip; wondering where he was going. They saw him walking arm in arm with a women whom they realised was his wife, Pilgrim called out to Chip.

"Don't forget to give us a bell!"

Chip stopped in the middle of the road and waved to the trio on the balcony calling out,

"I'll be in touch!"

They all waved back to Chip laughing and happy for him. Pilgrim watched Chip walk away down the high street, reunited with his formerly estranged wife, feeling very happy for him.

A sudden feeling of sorrow and regret it was all over pushed into his mind, although living with death as a constant companion had proved to be an ongoing nightmare.

Serving with comrades under such threatening circumstances had drawn them together as comrades in arms, forging a friendship that would last through an eternity. While Pilgrim felt a little sorry the escapade was at its end, he knew in his heart that all three of them were about to enjoy happier times.

As he waved again to his comrade, Pilgrim was realising this was a period when they were about to step into the sunnier side of life, out of the darkness and danger in which they had survived, to live normally once again.

These happy thoughts triggered the moving of his arm to pull Julie tightly to him. The big likeable lump Keyboard interrupted Pilgrim's thoughts as he shrugged his shoulders and said,

"I was right when I said this life is made up of heroes and fools, I like to think we're the heroes!"

Then Keyboard looked up from his musing and spoke to Pilgrim, with a quizzical look on his face,

"Oh by the way, Pilgrim who the hell is Horace?"

Julie and Pilgrim turned to look at each other—then burst out laughing!

THE END

EPILOGUE

Keyboard bought a luxury villa on the Costa Dell Sol in Spain to share with his new wife, Keyboard was so overcome with the guiding and stirring influence of the Grail; he attended church regularly, raising his family in a God fearing way.

Chip, well, he like Keyboard, lived a happy life with the love of his wife. Chip bought a business then just played at earning a living knowing he had plenty of money while enjoying the South Coast of England.

Pilgrim was welcomed back into the MI6 agencies, then treated like a hero; this obviously pleased his American parents. The newspapers offered large amounts of money for his story, but he was only interested in getting on with his life. After two years passed, he married Julie, then he looked forward to more adventures keeping England Safe!

As for the Knights Templars, they never heard from them again; so it was accepted by Pilgrim, Chip and Keyboard that the Holy Grail found its rightful owners.

PS.

Once in every two years the trio meet in the cafe on the anniversary of the day Chip met Pilgrim; who then accompanied him to the first meeting with the Satanist Tobias Friedman! Let it be further noted that the nickname Keyboard stuck with him for the rest of his days; while we certainly will not say anything more about Horace!

THE END